"You know you can trust me," Steve said.

"How? How do I know that, after everything that's happened?"

"Maybe because I want to get Rory back as much as you? Didn't you find anything in here," he whispered, touching her forehead, "to support my side of things?"

Afraid that the closeness of his body had impaired her speech, she could only shake her head.

"How about here?" He touched her breastbone, just above her heart.

It was an innocent enough connection, but he was so close and leaning closer that it set her thoughts off balance. His warm breath caressed her ear, sending a tremor through her senses.

"If you didn't really trust me, why did you ask for my help, Janie?"

Janie. She'd always loved it when he called her that. She felt her knees weaken, then mentally shook herself to get her wits back.

"I shouldn't have asked, but I thought you would help find..." Dear Lord, she'd nearly said "your son."

"Before we can go forward, Janie—" he probably knew what that name did to her "—you've got to believe I'm the only person who can help you."

ANGI MORGAN

HILL COUNTRY HOLDUP

HARLEQUIN®

TORONTO • NEW YORK • LONDON
AMSTERDAM • PARIS • SYDNEY • HAMBURG
STOCKHOLM • ATHENS • TOKYO • MILAN • MADRID
PRAGUE • WARSAW • BUDAPEST • AUCKLAND

Tim, thank you for encouraging me to follow my dream.

Recycling programs
for this product may
not exist in your area.

ISBN-13: 978-0-373-69499-0

HILL COUNTRY HOLDUP

Copyright © 2010 by Angela Platt

www.eHarlequin.com

Printed in U.S.A.

ABOUT THE AUTHOR

Angi Morgan had several jobs before taking the opportunity to stay home with her children and develop the writing career she always wanted. Volunteer work led to a houseful of visiting kids and an extended family. College breaks are full of homemade cookies, lots of visitors and endless hugs.

When the house is quiet, Angi plots ways to intrigue her readers with complex story lines. She throws her characters into situations they'll never overcome…until they find the one person who can help.

With their three children out of the house, Angi and her husband live in North Texas with only the four-legged "kids" to interrupt her writing. For up-to-date news and information, visit Angi at her Web site: www.AngiMorgan.com.

Books by Angi Morgan

HARLEQUIN INTRIGUE
1232—HILL COUNTRY HOLDUP

CAST OF CHARACTERS

Dr. Jane Palmer—With no roots of her own, she sought the security of a family for her son. But before she can introduce him to his father, Rory is kidnapped. She's willing to do anything to rescue her son—even run from the FBI.

Special agent Steve Woods—He refuses to let the Brant abduction end as badly as the case that haunts him. In order to save Thomas, he first must save Jane's son. Can he save both children and repair the broken relationship damaged by years of secrets?

Rory Palmer—Jane's son inherited her special gift, but needs his father's help to survive. Why is he the key to the Brant kidnapping?

Thomas Brant—The three-year-old son of a computer mogul kidnapped for a two million dollar ransom.

Special agent Roger McCaffrey—The leader of the CARD Team is on the hunt for a grieving mother involved in the kidnapping of Thomas Brant.

Agent George Lanning—Steve's partner is torn between their friendship and his job.

Agent Selena Stubblefield—Steve's former partner is willing to help Steve, but at what cost?

Dr. Hayden Hughes—Jane's closest friend. He's more than willing to play the role of Rory's father.

CARD Team—The FBI's Child Abduction Rapid Deployment Team.

Chapter One

Steve Woods focused on the woman pushing a million dollars through the Fourth of July spectators in Williams Square. They hadn't identified her yet. She'd taken possession of the stroller—and the hidden money—only four minutes ago.

Musical notes from the orchestra's "Baby Elephant Walk" faded into the background along with the chatter of the Texas crowd. His target swerved to the right so Steve ducked behind a double-wide plaid shirt, keeping out of her line of sight.

With the ease of a longtime mother, the suspect fussed over an imaginary baby. The Mustangs of Las Colinas sculpture loomed in the background as she stuffed the large bills into a pack she flung onto her shoulder.

The gut instinct that kept him alive through ten years of FBI fieldwork pumped adrenaline through his veins. He couldn't figure out what was wrong. But he would. Heart pounding, he searched for any sign of a weapon while wiping sweat from his forehead.

"Everyone count off." No one around him took notice that he spoke into a hidden microphone built into his earpiece. The bystanders appeared intent on following their noses, drawn by the aromas of funnel cakes, hamburgers and roasted corn. Or in grabbing the free samples of Starbucks coffee before the portable store packed up shop and went home. No one here knew that a little boy had been kidnapped.

"Greenback Two in position with a lock." George Lanning began the count. Only four out of the five followed.

"Where's Stubblefield? Does anyone have eyes on her position?"

"She was by the corn dog stand two minutes ago." Even without the help of his powerful scope, George had the best vantage point of the entire field from atop the north parking garage. "I can't find her ponytail."

"Greenbacks scramble. Switch to Bravo Tango Alpha," Steve said. The team changed frequencies to exclude Stubblefield in case her radio was compromised. "Granger, search her last position. I'm staying with the target."

The sun sank fast behind the surrounding buildings. Darkness was just as much their enemy as the kidnappers. Once the fireworks began, it would be hard keeping the woman in sight. They had to stay alert and not lose the target in the crowd, even while restrained to the meandering pace set by the woman pushing the stroller.

Wouldn't she be in a hurry to leave?

The money headed toward the middle of the activities, the center of a field of picnic blankets, lawn chairs and kids with glow-in-the-dark necklaces. Steve had his agents in place, but the large perimeter stretched their coverage. Their target was cut off completely by a man-made lake on the southeast side of the field. The kidnappers had chosen an ideal time and place to run their game.

"Where the heck is she going?"

"I've got nothing," George answered. "The monorail blocks my view of the other side of the lake. Who builds a lake in the middle of a business district anyway?"

"Apparently the city of Las Colinas," Winstrop mumbled.

"Cut the chatter," Steve commanded. "Keep your eyes open. Our area is overextended, and you guys know the Irving cops and highway patrol already have their hands full monitoring the crowd. Anyone see Stubblefield?" Blast it. Her first assignment after moving back to his team, and she wasn't following protocol. Terrific.

He needed to sort the facts and disconnect from the team's challenges. Thomas Brant Jr., son of the computer mogul, age twenty-nine months, had been snatched July 3 from his mother's arms just outside their Dallas home. One computer-generated note—free of fingerprints or any other identifying marks—left next to her unconscious body and broken arm. Intentionally broken by the monster abducting her son.

One million. Large bills. Unmarked.
Packed in small bag in kid's stroller.
Cover with blue blanket.
Williams Square, Irving Fireworks, 8:00 p.m.
No payment and he gets the same as the mother.

Their only lead was to follow the money.

Three adults and two children blocked Steve's view of the target. She stood five feet from the lake. He stood fifteen feet behind her, within his reach, but the sky was completely dark.

Time was up.

"Any word on Stubblefield?" Everyone rose or stopped walking as the national anthem began. Some placed their hands over their hearts, and some sang their pride off-key, especially the guy in front of him. Pushing his respect aside, he concentrated on the target. He could see the white of her knuckles from her tight grip on the guide bar of the stroller.

"I'm here," Stubblefield said, out of breath. "I'm trailing a suspicious teenager and lost radio contact."

"I no longer have a lock on the target," George interrupted. "Too many civilians in the way."

Steve inventoried his target—small frame, hair stuffed under a floppy hat, a drawstring bag looped over both shoulders, flip-flops, and a red, white and blue oversize shirt that hung to the edge of her tight, blue jean shorts.

Flip-flops?

Why would someone prepared to grab the money and run wear flip-flops?

The first rocket exploded. The hushed awe now shattered by the pops, sizzles and crackles of fireworks. Steve didn't let the noise distract him. He stared at the woman's slender ankles and bright red toenails. They moved.

Closer to the lake.

"She's going in the water!" he shouted to his team.

Shoving through two cowboys, he snatched the stroller. Frightened blue eyes turned to him. Familiar eyes.

It couldn't be…

A prick burned his forearm. He heard "I'm sorry" from a voice he remembered only too well. Her hands grabbed at his belt before he realized his knees had buckled and he crashed into her body. The ground meeting his shoulder didn't cause him pain, which was odd. There should have been a jolt.

Had he been shot?

A blurry image waved off the concerned men. The world swirled around him, lit by the white and silver rockets exploding over his head. Her hands shifted from his chest to the bag of money, where she unrolled…a hose? No, a breathing tube. She replaced the bag on her back as quickly as the shoes came off her feet.

"George." He struggled with words, unable to force his mouth or hands to move.

"He just collapsed," she told the men around her. Then she forced something into his hand. "I'm really sorry, Steve. Here's the antidote. The paralysis is only temporary."

Damn, it was his Jane. What was she doing here?

"I'll guide the paramedics here," she said, but he knew she wouldn't.

Dr. Jane Palmer, chemist, genius, ex-lover. Not exactly who he thought he'd be tracking tonight.

Barely able to turn his head, he caught sight of her sliding into the lake. No one paid any attention. The men were still shaking him, attempting to get a response. He couldn't move his pinkie, let alone follow. Jane disappeared in the water as the two guys trying to help him drew a crowd.

He struggled to keep his eyelids open. The guys shook him harder, as his team screamed "man down" and called for an ambulance. George shouted that the target was underwater and someone needed to follow her.

"Get out of the way!" Windstrom reached him first. The grass swished near Steve's ear before a friendly hand landed on his chest. "Woods? Can you hear me? Lanning, where are the EMTs? He's barely breathing."

"Where's he shot?"

"I can't find a wound." He pried Steve's fingers away from whatever Jane had placed in his fist. "Wait a minute. It's a note addressed to Zaphod? God, it's instructions to administer an antidote. There's a hypo here. Should I do it? George?"

Zaphod?

Steve heard the voices. Everything in his brain seemed to work, but he couldn't focus past the blur in his eyes or force his mouth to move.

He wasn't about to die until he figured out why and how Jane was involved in this kidnapping.

THANK GOD SHE COULD FIGURE out the breathing apparatus. If she had more than four minutes to make the underwater swim, Jane would question the motives of the universe. Question why the one man she prayed would rescue her, lay paralyzed from her drug 9RW6.

Special Agent Steve Woods. It had been almost four years.

She capped the flood of emotions that would block her from thinking clearly. She couldn't breathe from the pony tank and cry at the same time anyway. She kicked harder. Suppressed anger and frustration made her stronger with every stroke.

Rory needed her. Those bastards wouldn't hurt her son

because *she'd* made a mistake. Following the kidnapper's instructions, she continued through the dark water.

The kidnappers had kept her and Rory for the past two days, keeping her awake and drilling their plan into her mind. The only chance Rory had was for her to follow their instructions. They'd taken her formula and forced her to use it against whoever chased her from the plaza. And great, it had to be Steve and the FBI. Did they know about Rory's kidnapping? Was that why Steve was there?

Maybe he'd be taken off the case, and she wouldn't have to deal with him. Anyone but him. She couldn't handle his explanations or accusations. Not now. She hadn't expected Steve to be there tonight but maybe they'd understand the note faster if he was involved. He would know what her cryptic message meant.

Wouldn't he?

They were the FBI, for pity's sake. *God help me.* She prayed with each stroke that carried her closer to one of her son's abductors.

Fear nipped at her system and caused her breath to hitch. Not good while trying to breathe underwater. Better to concentrate on the rhythm of her strokes, on her strength. On how she would methodically tear the kidnappers limb from limb if they harmed her little boy. They would wish they had killed her if anything happened to Rory.

Any time now. Bringing the illuminated diving compass closer to her goggles, she cautiously surfaced at the instructed coordinates. Exploding fireworks cast enough flickering light to see a black-clad figure steering a small rowboat about fifteen feet away.

A man wearing a pull-on President Clinton mask hauled her over the side. She wasn't seated properly before he threw a towel in her direction and wrenched the heavy bag from her back. His deranged laughter made her spine shudder.

"I don't care what the money is for, it doesn't matter.

Just don't hurt Rory. I'll do anything to get my son back."

Anything.

"Clinton" ignored her plea and threw a lumpy grocery sack at her feet. Huddling under the dark towel, she pulled yet another tight stretchy shirt over her head. For the second phase in this nightmare to work, she needed to appear dry while driving away.

Separate yourself from the emotion, Jane. Her mother's voice rang clear. Panic never resolved anything. The one time she'd thrown caution to the wind, her sense of freedom had left her pregnant and raising a child alone.

She ignored the putrid pond stench and the rubbery feeling in her legs from swimming the race of her life. Once they reached shore, her captor held a Glock in his gloved hand. There weren't too many people on this side of the lake by the parking garage. None close enough to notice her or the man in the Clinton mask.

Now that they had what they wanted, she assumed the gunman wouldn't hesitate to shoot. So she obeyed her instructions by not calling out for help or drawing attention to herself.

They climbed over a half wall that formed the ground floor of a dimly lit parking garage. A car sat three spaces from the exit.

Judging from the vivid colors bursting in the sky and the John Philip Sousa melody echoing across the lake, the program had reached its finale. She needed to be in traffic when the fireworks ended.

"Clinton" tossed her the keys. Without a grunt in her direction, the guy took off. She had no idea what he looked like. She couldn't identify anything about him except his average height and slender build.

Helpless.

That summed everything up. She couldn't prove anything, give the police anything to go on, or assist in any way. The creep hadn't even spoken to her. The abductors' instructions were burned into her memory.

She popped the trunk and settled a long blond wig complete with dark roots onto her head. The walk alongside the car took a minute with new bright orange flip-flops on her feet. She pulled the seat forward as others began loading their cars with lounge chairs and coolers.

Adjusting the mirrors, she tried to achieve a bored look, and desperately tried to slow the beat of her heart. No use. She pulled out of the Omni Hotel's garage. Despite her best efforts, her protective bubble of self-control lay close to shattering. Willpower alone kept her alert, despite appearing relaxed behind the steering wheel. Her insides churned as if she were the contents of a giant milkshake.

The stream of automobiles thickened. She passed policeman after policeman directing traffic. The urge to scream for help grew until she had to cover her mouth with a shaking hand.

The cars came to a complete stop in all directions, and an ambulance siren screamed through the intersection. Guilt rattled her, creating another crack in her discipline. Steve. They must be moving him to a hospital, but he'd be okay. He had to be okay.

Breathe in. Breathe out. Hold on to the steering wheel. Follow directions. She steadily moved her hands to a ten-and-two position on the hard cool plastic.

Everything will work out. Follow the plan.

With or without Steve's help identifying her, the FBI would connect the antidote to Dr. Jane Palmer, research scientist. During the past two days, she hadn't been given an opportunity to contact the police or Steve. Now she was a fugitive, part of the kidnappers' plan. If she called anyone for help, she couldn't save Rory.

Every person she knew would be interrogated. Her home would be invaded, and everything she owned would be searched. They'd find the book. Now that Steve was part of this, there was a good chance they'd understand the clue that much sooner.

Please God. Bring my little boy back to me. She prayed over and over and over.

Heading westbound on Highway 114, she eased her foot off the accelerator as she passed a black-and-white. The lake house would be there no matter how fast she drove.

"You have to pull through this, Steve. We need your help."

THREE HOURS IN THE HOSPITAL and still no one knew what had happened to him. He'd been informed they'd found another antidote vial locked in a safe at her apartment. Antidote for what? Everyone wanted to know but Jane held all the answers. It was her serum.

Determined to leave, he'd forced his doctor to admit that nothing was seriously wrong with him. He pulled his shirt over his head just as George came through the curtains.

"Has the Brant kid shown?"

"We lost her." His partner dropped his eyes to the floor and shook his head.

"You've got a team finding out where she's working?" he asked and tucked his shirt into his jeans.

"You ordered that as soon as you could talk." George frowned and scratched his scalp. "Of course, we followed through. We know she rented a car yesterday."

Steve slipped his left foot into a boot and bent to pull it on. He nearly lost what little was left in his stomach but wasn't sharing that bit of info with anyone. He wanted out of the hospital and on the trail of the kidnappers. And Jane.

He pulled on the second boot and sat straight again, forcing a shaky hand to smooth back his hair before he slipped on his Stetson.

"Palmer sure caught us with our pants down," George said. "It was like she knew we were shorthanded."

"Maybe. But…" He couldn't believe it. Jane wasn't a kidnapper.

"But?"

But with a stick from her needle, she'd paralyzed him and left. What should he believe? "Just find her."

"I'm driving you home." George dug his hands into his jeans pockets and shifted from foot to foot. "Come on, Steve. We've got this covered."

"I know Jane Palmer."

"You didn't even know she was back in town, man. According to the landlord, she's been here six weeks."

No, he hadn't known she was back. And he didn't know where she lived, but he did know Jane. He knew every inch of her body, every inch of her soul. She couldn't be a part of the kidnapping. But she had to be since she'd picked up the ransom. He had very little time to determine why.

The doctor warned him to take it easy for the next several days as he left the hospital. As if he actually would. A kid was still missing. And his ex-lover was climbing the FBI's most wanted list.

George punched the unlock button for the F150. "I can't take you anywhere but home, Steve. Orders."

"Who's in charge?" He climbed in, still stiff from the drug.

"McCaffrey. He knows about your history with Jane. You're on official medical leave until they know exactly what that serum did to you. Among other unanswered questions."

Like how he was involved. "Are they through at her apartment?"

"Don't do this to yourself, man."

"What would you do?" He yanked the Stetson to his lap and rested his throbbing head against the seat.

"She left you, Steve. She packed up and moved after two words—*good* and *bye*."

George started the engine. A light rain distorted the oncoming headlights. Steve leaned his aching forehead on the cool side window.

"It was a bit more complicated than that," he said quietly, his thoughts being thrust back four years to a time he'd rather block from his memory.

"You can come with me," Jane had said calmly. He could hear the disbelief in her voice. Disbelief that he encouraged her to follow her dream, to take a job offer that didn't come along twice in a lifetime.

"It's not that easy, honey. I'd have to wait for an opening to transfer. I'd lose my place on the team. You know what's coming up. This is the undercover break I wanted. It may be months before you hear from me, and I can't let you—"

"Don't say it, Steve. Don't tell me I've got to live up to my potential. Don't say you won't stand in my way."

"What kind of a life would we have here? I'm gone months at a time. You'd spend hours in a lab doing mindless work. You'd choose that kind of life over your dream job? You've been dying for this opportunity."

"You figured all this out on your own. No discussion?"

"I belong here, hon." He pulled her into his arms.

"And what about us?" Her hands went around his waist, holding on to him like a lifeline.

He held her, never wanting to let go, but knowing it was the best he could do at the moment. "We can't forget about everything we've both worked—"

She cut his stupid words off with a kiss. One that released every emotion bottled up inside him. Their lovemaking was exquisite, unhurried and all night.

And in the end, she'd left.

The opportunity at Johns Hopkins was too important and prestigious to pass up. If she'd stayed in Dallas, she would have regretted it the rest of their lives. He'd gone undercover posing for the next five months as a husband desperate to adopt a child. His team had run the sting trying to stop the illegal sale of abducted children.

Nothing had gone right. His cover had been blown. They'd lost track of the kids. He still wasn't over that.

But their breakup had been for the best. Jane hadn't written from Baltimore. He hadn't heard from her. Not even an e-mail. He couldn't blame Jane for leaving. He'd pushed her out the door.

Another person gone. But this one had come back and hadn't called. She'd made her choice.

Enough said.

It took twenty minutes to get to his house, but only ten to get Jane's address from George. It was close to the University of Texas campus in Arlington. Close to where she'd lived when she'd been in school. Close to where they'd met.

Okay, pal. Build a bridge and get over it. Keep a level head or you'll give the brass a reason to keep you off the case even longer.

Feeling like warmed-over cow patties, he should have stayed home. But this was Jane.

His gut told him two plus two just didn't add up to four. Flashing his badge at the officer still at the scene, he ducked under the crime scene tape and entered the totally wrecked apartment. There hadn't been any reason for his team to be gentle.

Stacks of empty cutesy frames that had filled every nook of her apartment four years ago were dumped from boxes as if she hadn't unpacked. Jane loved pictures, but she had a habit of buying the frame and forgetting to print the picture to fill it. The knickknacks cluttering the top shelves matched everything he remembered. Nails, but no pictures on the walls. Nothing on the lower shelves.

One bedroom remained completely empty. Odd. The desk was in the living area. Why get a two-bedroom if you're going to put your desk inconveniently by the patio door? Didn't make sense. Jane was a scientist and couldn't live without having access to her files and external hard drive. So where was the computer? She hauled the entire PC with her on a kidnapping?

He still couldn't believe she was involved.

The same comforter she'd had since she was eleven lay bunched in the middle of her bed. That was more like her—a creature of habit. During their three months together it had been hard to get her to change any routine.

That uncomfortable feeling crept up the back of his neck again. The feeling he got when things were about to go from bad to worse.

Upturned bureau drawers cluttered the floor. Clothes were piled under them. He picked up a picture of a very young Jane with her mother. She still had big sad eyes, as if she carried the fate of the world on her shoulders. Just one lone picture?

It didn't make sense.

Still slender with dark auburn hair, she hadn't changed. Well, her bangs were dark. That was all he'd seen under that cap. He ran his finger over her lips. They'd still be soft and luscious.

Opening the drawer in the nightstand, he found the book. Just one. A very used copy of *The Hitchhiker's Guide to the Galaxy.*

Jackpot.

It had been a challenge to find a book she'd never read. A book she couldn't quote by heart. He didn't need to open the cover to see the words written inside, but he did anyway. "My favorite book is yours. Love, Steve." He'd struggled with the words long enough, wanting them to be meaningful, yet casual.

He'd come here specifically to find this, just in case the reference to one of its characters in his "antidote note" hadn't been a fluke. He flipped through the pages, finding a Valentine's Day card with last year's date and a "Love, Hayden."

Who was Hayden?

Under the card was a picture of Jane and himself at his

parents' lake house. He flipped it over. *Austin Lake Country where Steve assured me I wasn't alone in the galaxy.*

She'd kept the book and his picture.

Dr. Jane Palmer closely guarded a secret about herself. He'd given her his favorite book for her birthday present, then found out she had an amazing memory. She could recite chapters of books she'd read in college.

Shoot, he couldn't go down memory lane right now. But he could go exactly where Jane had pointed him. Lake Buchanan, near Austin.

He pulled out his cell and had his thumb over the speed dial for George. It was more than a hunch now. Jane had deliberately left him a trail. She needed him.

But why not call the FBI? Why not write on the antidote note that she was in trouble? Why "Zaphod"? Because he'd understand immediately, and no one else would.

What if he were wrong? McCaffrey would have his head if he misdirected the team. He didn't want to be permanently relieved of duty. Right?

He brought up the directory and retrieved the number for Southwest Airlines. If he were lucky, he could catch the first plane to Austin and bring Jane in alone. It was the safest way to get her to turn herself in and sort out why she was working with kidnappers.

What did he have to lose?

NINE TEDIOUS HOURS and Jane was losing her patience. Driving to Lake Buchanan through heavy rains had been a nightmare. Unexpected flooding in south Texas shut down roads and delayed her by four hours.

Her uncanny recall for details had set her apart for as long as she could remember. But an eidetic memory didn't help in storms that obliterated the road signs or detours due to flooding.

How she'd wished for her ability to go away so she could

be like normal little girls. A normal life full of dolls, playtime and friends. Full of stability instead of university studies. That "special" part of her everyone admired had contributed to her exploitation by her parents, losing her dream job and now the kidnapping of her son.

The formula stored in her unique memory had drawn criminal attention to her. Guess she didn't blend in well enough after all. If she had, Rory would be safe at home instead of in the hands of coldhearted kidnappers.

Thunder echoed across the landscape, jolting her back to the driving rain beating against the windshield. It had started storming south of Stephenville and never let up. Kingsland had received its share, too. Although it was nearly seven in the morning, the sky remained shrouded in darkness as the rain continued to pour.

She drove past two barricades on the last turn and parked the car in a drive leading to an unused field. The ground was normally a mixture of small pebbles and dirt, but was now mainly water and mud. A couple of steps from the car and she slid to the ground, losing the flip-flops in the dark. She walked the last quarter mile to the lake house, falling time and again.

Her luck had to change. If the FBI understood her message, she could wait for their help here, away from the kidnappers' view.

If they didn't show, she'd get a message to them. Somehow. But she was too exhausted to think after driving all night. And if Steve decided to come, what then? She'd thought about how to break the news to him. He deserved to know. But how did you tell a man he was a father and that his son had been kidnapped in the same sentence?

I can't think anymore. She finally sloshed up the muddy walkway thankful the heavy rains had placed the lake country in a flash-flood warning. There weren't any cars along the road or in the driveway. No lights on in the house. Hopefully, the family was still at the ranch.

Amanda Woods, Steve's mother, usually hid a key so her kids could use their weekend retreat at a moment's notice. Jane hoped it would be that way now, or she'd spend a horrible wet day in the boathouse. She hooked the soggy strands from the wig behind her ears, wearing it just in case someone saw her or if she was stopped.

She pulled the key from under Brandon's Texas-shaped stone near the roses, meaning Steve's brother had been the last one here. They each had a cement rock with their handprint and initials from when they were five.

Walking along the veranda-style porch, she wondered what it would have been like to have a loving family with traditions and roots. Her parents had done what they thought was best, protecting her from…well, everything. Yet exposing her to one university study after another and keeping her from a normal childhood.

To be normal was all she wanted for Rory. And now? One step at a time. Or one hurdle.

The door swung open without a squeak. Now breaking and entering could be added to her list of fugitive accomplishments.

Trembling from nerves more than the damp, she grabbed a towel from the shelf in the mudroom and buried her face in its softness. A good sleep was far beyond her reach without Rory in her arms. But she'd been up for days and craved to stretch out with a pillow under her head. Just for an hour or so.

"Fancy meeting you here."

Jane screamed, dropped the terry cloth, and looked up to see Steve. A very alive, strong, healthy Steve. Goose bumps broke out across her flesh at the intensity of his stare. She took a deep breath, calming her racing blood.

The T-shirt stretched taut across his muscular chest. He looked great. Too perfect for words. But she could come up with a few: *absolute, excellent, flawless, hunk, masterful.* Not to mention *archaic, pig-headed* and *loner.*

Steve's brow wrinkled, and the tiny laugh lines around his eyes were emphasized. She'd been gaping at him, but couldn't help another look down his long, lean torso and back up again to his lightly whiskered face. Another gaze at the last and only man she wanted to see.

But, dear God in heaven, she'd missed everything about him. The shape of his once-broken nose, his deep brown eyes, how his dark hair curled out from under his hat—even his boots. She wanted to throw herself into his arms but couldn't. He'd made his choice four years ago. Having him hold her wouldn't change that.

"You look surprised to see me." He blocked the door leading into the rest of the house. He was dry and immaculate except for that little bit of stubble that drove her crazy. "Didn't you leave me a note?"

Technically she'd left two. "I expected someone else." She wasn't up to verbally sparring with him. She wanted to warm up and dry off. Curl up and cry. Turn everything over to the FBI and be certain they'd find Rory.

"Yeah, well, that knockout juice left a heckuva hangover." He rubbed his forehead while continuing. "But I managed to make a plane."

"Just you? None of your team is here? Why wouldn't they come? You never work alone."

"I take orders *from* the FBI, or at least I think I do." He rubbed his temples again. "They put me on medical leave after I was stuck with an unknown drug."

"You were obviously injected with the antidote so you have nothing to worry about." She needed to sit down. She pushed at his chest, attempting to get around him, but he held his ground, not budging from the mudroom.

"You know, for a genius you're not making much sense. You left a note for me to follow, but you're surprised to see me." He shoved the dripping blond wig off her head, resting his hands on her shoulders. "What's going on, Jane? If something's wrong, why not just tell the authorities everything?"

"It was the only thing I could come up with. There wasn't a way to write a note." She didn't dare look at him again. She kept her eyes focused on the scuff marks on his boots. She was just too shaky to think straight. "The picture was already in the book, so I decided to come here and hope."

"Why tell the FBI where you were going at all? Kidnapping has serious consequences. Tell me where the boy is and where you stashed the money."

"What are you talking about?" She'd kidnapped someone and had the money? "The kidnappers said they'd give him back if I did what they asked."

His hands stilled and created two pools of warmth through her wet T-shirt.

She opened her mouth to ask about Rory but couldn't. He let her go and turned away. But not before she'd seen the disappointment on his face. The same disappointment she experienced for not having enough courage to tell him about Rory.

Steve pulled his cell from his belt. "I've got to call McCaffrey and let him know I'm bringing you in."

"I can't go back to Dallas!"

"Oh, yes, you can. I don't know how you got involved, but—"

She tried to take the cell from his hand. His grip was too firm so she kept her fingers wrapped around his. "Please, Steve, I need you to listen to me."

"It's a kidnapping." He shook her hand from his, but didn't dial the phone. "Every minute counts if we're going to find the kid."

"The kid? His name is Rory." So he didn't know. But why was he there? She couldn't tell him about his son like this. She needed to think. Plan what and how. She hadn't really slept in three days. Everything was getting jumbled in her head.

"Rory?" He wrinkled his brow. "You collected the ransom for Thomas Brant. The kid you and a couple of monsters abducted yesterday morning."

Another kidnapping? A second little boy was missing? She stumbled against the washer and slowly slid to the floor.

Sweet mother of God, would she ever see her son again?

Chapter Two

"Are you okay?" Steve's first instinct was to kneel down and pull Jane into his arms, but he couldn't. She was a fugitive.

Wanted for kidnapping.

And no longer his.

"I'm so stupid." Her hands covered her face and she burst into tears. More than tears. Her body shook from the force. She rocked back and forth like a woman keening for a lost child.

This near hysterical person was not the woman he had known four years ago. Jane hadn't shed a tear as they parted ways or at any point in their relationship.

"I'll never see...him...again," she hiccupped.

"What in the world are you talking about?"

"My son, Rory. He's gone. They took him. I can't believe I... Oh, my God."

When he couldn't watch the stream of tears any longer, he knelt until she looked him in the eyes. "I don't think I heard you right, Jane. You keep saying your son. The little boy that's missing is Thomas Brant."

"And Rory. They have Rory."

"You're saying they kidnapped two kids and one is yours?" He got back to his feet.

Her bottom lip trembled and her head dropped as she pulled her knees in close to her chest again.

Steve couldn't have heard her correctly. He'd been up

all night, drugged yesterday and his brain wasn't working right. Were her words just the result of a drug-induced hallucination?

She had a son? Jane? His Jane?

Her dark auburn hair was plastered to her scalp, she was soaked to the skin, but she was still beautiful with those tear-filled eyes staring up at him. And very real.

Leaning on the doorjamb kept him upright, but he couldn't think. He forced his hand to reach out. After a few seconds her shivering fingers wrapped around his and he pulled her to her bare, muddy feet. Then he moved, taking the short tiled hall in four steps with Jane following. He tossed his phone onto a chair, sinking onto its match. All his energy had been zapped right out of him when he heard those words.

She had a son.

"Why didn't you tell me?" He croaked the question past a very dry throat, wanting to head to his dad's wet bar and the bottle of Jim Bean hidden from view. "When did you get married?"

That guy was lucky. Jane was smart, beautiful and crazy in bed. He couldn't think of her like that. The hell he couldn't. She'd been with him first. *Her* kid was missing on top of being involved with the Brant kidnapping. *Pull yourself together, Woods. You made your choice four years ago.*

"His father is… He's… I wanted to call you, Steve." She closed her eyes and drew a deep breath. "I couldn't tell you. They said not to involve any police or the FBI. I couldn't risk it."

"Wait, slow down. Let's start at the beginning."

If he couldn't have a shot of whiskey, he might as well make it aspirin. Where did his mom keep them? He pushed out of the chair and stretched his stride to its limit, but stopped short of the kitchen.

"The beginning? Rory and I were going to the park."

"Why didn't you tell me you had a kid?"

"Why do you think you had the right to know? I thought

it was better to just keep things the way you wanted." She sat
on the couch, looking as completely worn-out as he felt, but
the words still managed to sting. "You were undercover and
couldn't be reached."

Undercover for almost three years. A lot had happened to
her while his life had been on hold.

"I thought we were friends." Yeah, he knew the futility of
the words as they left his mouth and didn't need it confirmed
by her look of you're-just-being-stupid. "Don't you think a
significant thing like having a kid warrants a phone call?"

"The phone works both ways, buddy. You never called me,
either."

The truth flicked him like a bullwhip, inflicting small sharp
pangs of guilt. Yeah, he could have found her. He had ways,
contacts. But he'd avoided admitting his culpability, and then
it seemed too late for a relationship.

"Wait a minute," he said. "I couldn't call you while I was
undercover. You knew that."

"I tried to write several times, but what could I say? You
made your feelings very clear when you asked me to leave."
Sniffing, she draped a worn afghan around her, like a protective wall between them.

"Who's the father? Could he be involved?" Probably some
genius guy she worked with. It had to be. Maybe that Hayden
fellow?

His desire to think superseded the need for aspirin so he
skimmed the perimeter of the room, pacing as far away from
the afghan and what it covered as possible. He didn't want to
recall the disappointment he'd experienced and just how much
he'd wanted a letter during that first assignment. If he did
admit it, that would mean he'd been wrong. No, his work over
the past four years had been important. It wasn't a waste.

Jane's hand peeked from under the blanket to brush her
hair back. "His dad's never been involved with him. And he'd
be the last person to kidnap a small child."

So, the guy had been after sex and not the consequences. Jane deserved better.

As if she thought the same, she pushed off the couch, dragging the afghan around her shoulders to the window. "We have to find Rory."

Lightning glistened off the phone in the chair, beckoning him to do his job. He should call his team. It was important to let McCaffrey know he had the suspect. Or he could get Jane's story, then make the call since the FBI needed information on her son's kidnapping.

"When did you get back to Dallas?"

There hadn't been any evidence of a child living in Jane's apartment. Could he be wrong? Could all this just be a ruse to throw him off? After all, he hadn't seen her in years. But why leave a note he was certain to follow?

"Ten days ago." Jane leaned against the window frame and looked expectantly out toward the lake.

Her landlord had told them six weeks.

"No one else is coming," he said. *At least no one* I'm *expecting.* "Why would someone kidnap your son? What would they gain?"

"I wasn't looking for anyone." She seemed more resigned, more somber if that were possible. "The new drugs I'm developing are very valuable. The sedative is what I used on you yesterday."

"It has a heck of a kick."

"It's not fully developed. I wasn't scheduled to begin at the lab until Monday. Copies of the formula and several vials were still at the apartment. They took everything."

Wrapped tightly in the afghan, she took small steps back to the couch and perched on the edge.

"How would they know about it?"

"My money's from the private sector. It came after my paper was published in the *Journal of Anesthesiology.* Anyone could know about it."

"What about your dream job at Johns Hopkins? Did they have any right to the research?"

"Actually, that job didn't work out. I've been privately funded with the understanding that my research belongs to me. So I have a lot of control over the development of the drugs. At least for the time being."

"Was there a bidding war? Did someone get pissed off because you cut them out of the deal? Maybe another partner?"

"I worked alone and approached a friend at Foster Pharmaceuticals. It wasn't associated with anyone or any company."

"We're getting ahead of ourselves," he said. "Tell me what happened with your son."

Taking a deep breath, she dropped her head onto the back of his mother's old couch cushions, closed her eyes and pushed her hair behind her ears. "God, I can't believe this is really happening."

Another deep breath and a long pause. He wanted to ask a million questions, but his Bureau training held firm. He slowly sat back in the chair across from her to wait on the story. Waiting was the worst part of his job.

"Mrs. Newinsky, my neighbor on the floor below, greeted us when the movers pulled up to the building last week. She constantly came over and offered to watch Rory. We were going to grill hot dogs at the park July second, but she forgot to buy a package of buns."

A tear fell from her right eye, and she swiped it away as if it never existed.

"I didn't think twice. I just thought it would be quicker if I went to the store and she stayed with Rory." Jane sat forward and picked lint from the afghan with trembling fingers, avoiding his gaze. There was a small sniff. Then her eyes met his, but she quickly looked out the window where the rain continued to pour.

"I…um…" She struggled, swallowing hard. "I got back and

they were inside my apartment. At least two of them. With guns. They never spoke, wore masks and shoved typed notes in front of me."

Steve forced himself not to interrupt and then pried his short nails from the palms of his hands. He stood, needing to relax, keep a clear head and not tear her story apart. Just let her finish.

"Mrs. Newinsky and Rory weren't there. The note had instructions telling me they had Rory and they'd take me to him if I didn't make a scene."

"So that happened two days before I followed you at the fireworks."

"I didn't have a choice. I had to do what they said. They had Rory. I got into the side door of a black van and didn't see the plates. They blindfolded me—"

"Did you count the turns? Any unusual smells or sounds?"

"As much as I would like to believe I could re-create the ride, I tried to keep track but I can't tell you anything significant. It was a building with no visible address. I couldn't see the surrounding skyline. Nothing. All I know is that forty-something turns later I still wasn't with Rory."

"What did they want?"

"Not much the first day. Being separated from Rory drove me insane. It was the same for most of July third."

"Wait a minute. You rented a car on the third."

"Not me." She shook her head and pulled the afghan tighter. "The last note said the car was in my name and to avoid the police. It also stated to find the stroller by the Mustang sculpture at the fireworks. Everything I needed, including clothes, was in the car. One man drove me to the hotel parking garage."

Images of a little boy floated into his mind, a toddler with short chubby legs and a patch of light brown hair the shade of Jane's.

Why was he unable to concentrate? He was a federal agent.

He should be able to keep his head, be able to think about this situation rationally. He diligently concentrated on the tile where each boot fell as he paced.

"How many men were there?"

"I think two, but it's hard to be certain."

"Could you recognize any of them?" His boot hit a cracked tile. An accident he and his brother were probably responsible for. *Concentrate.*

"They wore full head masks and never spoke."

"Since they didn't do anything to you and didn't need you earlier than the fourth, why not wait and take you just before the fireworks? Why take your son? Why this elaborate scheme to collect ransom money?"

She didn't answer. Didn't look at him. Didn't shrug or move. Then her chin quivered.

He felt like an ass.

"So tell me about last night."

"They watched everything I did during the fireworks. The one time they spoke, their voices were altered somehow. One guy met me in a boat, took the money and took me to the car. I needed to hide, so I came here on the way to San Antonio."

"San Antonio?"

"That's what the instructions said to do. I need to meet them at the Alamo on the sixth and I'll get Rory back."

No spoken instructions? Disappearing notes? Secret formulas and threats to her child? This was so farfetched he didn't know where to begin to tear her story to shreds. It didn't make sense.

And what happens if she's lying to you, pal? A niggling voice kept gnawing at his thoughts. There weren't any pictures, no kid clothes, no toys.

"I went to your apartment, Jane." Confronting her was easier than playing guessing games. "There isn't any evidence to support what you're telling me."

"What do you mean?"

Like he would with any suspect, he watched for tells. Subtle expression changes, a shifting of her eyes to indicate she was lying.

All he could see was Jane. Holy cow, she wasn't lying. She had a son. Rory was real.

"The team wasn't gentle when they searched your place, but they were thorough. I think I would have noticed if a child lived there."

Jane looked confused. "Why would they take his things? It was the only room I'd finished unpacking."

The tip of Jane's nose turned red from holding back the tears she refused to surrender to again. Her lip trembled as much as her clasped hands. He clenched his jaw tighter to withhold his sympathy and drew on a reserve of professionalism he'd never tapped before.

This wasn't a normal abduction. It didn't fit any profile, any standard he could focus on. His gut told him the kidnappers didn't have any intention of returning her son. It didn't make sense.

"Who are these ghosts?" He didn't hold back his frustration, letting his voice boom through the room. She flinched. He didn't expect Jane to answer, but she shrugged and choked back a sob.

"I don't know. I didn't see them." She dropped her face into her hands, thought better of it and looked into the far corner. "Details scream at me every moment of my life. I don't forget anything. Ever. But I can't remember what they didn't expose me to."

"I want to believe you." But he wouldn't let his wants get in the way of reality. As much as he wanted to accept everything she said, he still hadn't heard a viable reason why she would be anyone's target. The Brants, yes. They had a million dollars' worth of reasons—that Jane didn't have with her anymore.

"How did you know I'd find your message?"

"Actually, I hoped they wouldn't have to involve you, Steve. I assumed the police would discover who I am and hoped. I *hoped* that someone would look inside the book."

Dang it! Did all her actions imply she was innocent or did he *want* her to be? "Why not just write details about the kidnapping and let the police know about your son?"

"They handed the note to me when we arrived in the parking garage. I found the stroller, then found a free pen when I passed by a booth. I barely managed to write 'Zaphod' on the top before the fireworks began. I hoped by mentioning a character from your favorite book, it would draw your attention to the case. What if they don't follow through, Steve? I need your help to make certain I'm the one at the Alamo."

With McCaffrey in charge, there wasn't much chance of him helping with the exchange. He had serious doubts anything he said would be taken into consideration.

"Driving here wasn't the smartest thing to do, Jane." The rain had probably played in her favor, or she would have been apprehended in that rental. Which was probably what the kidnappers had wanted. "You should have called me, the police, anyone who could have helped you."

With her body covered with the afghan, he couldn't pick up any abnormal nervousness. She had just as much apprehension as any parent he'd interviewed after a child went missing.

"When we were together, Steve, you spoke of your last case. The reason you were on medical leave. The parents didn't follow the kidnappers' instructions—" a choked sob caught in her throat "—and the child…"

Died.

He remembered Kevin Haughton every day. He couldn't avoid seeing the scar on his chest from the bullet that had nearly killed him. There wasn't any way on earth he could argue with her reasoning. He'd given it to her.

"I couldn't take the chance to phone on the way here. What if they were following me? I thought I was doing the best thing."

"I don't doubt you thought you were right. But this makes no sense. Kidnappers don't work this way. Why involve another person? Why *you?* Why force you to pick up the ransom from a second abduction?" He walked the length of the living room.

Stopping at the window, he watched the steady downpour of rain. Rising water would soon be their enemy, just like time. The longer the kidnappers took to return her son, the less likely he'd be found.

God, he was convinced. It surprised him how easily Jane had persuaded him. Yet, he knew she was holding something back.

"What's next?" he asked her. "You said you were waiting to surface in San Antonio. When?"

"I need to be at the Alamo tomorrow morning at ten. They're supposed to give me Rory," she said.

Steve heard another choked sob, and his chest constricted tighter.

During their whirlwind romance, Jane had never cried. Their days and nights had been completely filled with laughter and love. Keeping his back to her now and maintaining his distance was one of the most difficult things he'd ever done. He tightened his grip on the window frame, but could only focus on her reflected image in the glass as she slipped the blanket from her shoulders. No woman's tears had ever affected him this way.

"Steve—" her voice shook near the point of breaking "—you said the other little boy hadn't been returned. Does that mean they won't…that they may hurt Rory?"

Turning to her, he tried to reassure her, refusing to think about the possibilities connected to this strange MO. He wouldn't stop until he found both boys. "He'll be fine. We'll find them both."

"But—"

"No buts. We'll leave as soon you can get some of Mom's clothes and shoes, before the flooding gets worse." He looked pointedly at the towel around her neck and smiled as reassuringly as he could. "The phone is out. I need to try my cell again since I couldn't get a signal earlier."

"What will happen if the police think I kidnapped the Bran child?" Her eyes widened and pleaded as she shook her head. "You can't tell them I'm with you, Steve. Promise me. Rory needs me."

"I promise to do everything I can to find him."

She rose and the towel fell behind her as she walked to him with her shoulders back and face tilted to look him in the eyes. Her small hand flattened on his chest covering his heart. The rest of her body followed until he could rest his chin on the top of her head. He wanted to kiss her so badly he could barely get air into his lungs.

Would he ever be able to think straight around her?

"Please tell me I'm doing the right thing by trusting you," she whispered. "They said not to let the FBI know, but I need you. I can't do this alone."

He put his arms around her, loving every miserable minute of agony it caused him. At that moment he didn't care if it would jeopardize the operation. He didn't care if his attachment was too strong and would cloud his judgment. He wanted Jane right where she was.

"We've got to call. It's our only choice, Jane. Dallas doesn't have any leads except you." He let his words hang in the air a moment, but she didn't respond. "They don't know your neighbor is missing. If we find her, she may be able to give a description of the kidnappers."

"I can't let you take me back." Barely shaking her head, she tightened her grip on his shirt. "Not until I've done what they said I have to do." Her body trembled, an imperceptible tremor that could be associated with tears.

"It's okay to cry, Jane," he whispered in her ear.

"No, it's not. It achieves nothing and keeps me from thinking. But I miss Rory. What if he's scared and is crying for me?"

"You can't think of that." He could say the same for himself. It impaired an agent's judgment when he got too involved.

Like he was right now, cradling Jane. "We have to concentrate on getting him back. And we will. I promise."

But he couldn't make promises that excluded the best way to find the Brant kid. Somehow, he'd contact his team *and* protect Jane. By harboring and abetting a suspected felon? Him. Steve Woods, hard-nosed, by-the-book FBI agent.

Yeah, shot down with one look from the only woman who'd ever meant anything to him.

Chapter Three

The storm raged outside. Whitecaps on the lake splashed over the boat dock. A perfect scene for Jane's turbulent feelings and emotions. She was drowning in guilt. Guilt over leaving Rory, guilt over not telling Steve straightaway he was a father.

Even now, she couldn't wrap her mind around any words good enough to explain why she'd waited so long to tell him. Nothing she formed in her mind convinced her to say the words aloud.

"What's he like?" Steve asked near the top of her head.

"Rory?" She couldn't breathe. Of all the things he could have asked, she wasn't prepared to describe his son to him. Not right now.

"Yeah, Rory. Your son."

Your son. Simple words she didn't know how to correct. The lie gave her a nauseous feeling. His son, too. Was it too late to tell him?

Just do it. Say, "Steve, you're Rory's father." Tell him why you kept his son away from him for almost four years. Tell him you were an idiot and scared to death of losing everything. Tell him why you came back to Texas.

Tell him!

"I thought you said you needed to make a call," she said instead, too much of a coward to try to convince Steve of anything else.

"Calling will wait."

Jane searched his face for Agent Steve Woods. He was as reliable as a Swiss Army knife when it came to the Bureau. He'd never put off work before. He'd chosen his job over a possible future with her.

Granted, four years ago they'd only been together several weeks and he'd been between assignments. But the fervor he'd used when talking about his job made her more than a little envious.

She'd yearned for that passion. It was part of what drew her to him. It would be so nice to get lost in Steve's enthusiasm for life. To forget about all her worries for just a little while. But Rory's kidnapping was her first priority.

Lightning lit the sky and thunder shook the windows. The weather wasn't working in her favor. The longer she waited to tell him the truth, the less he'd believe her. What would he say when she admitted she'd kept knowledge of his child from him?

"Maybe this conversation should wait. It's getting worse out there." He nodded his head toward the window. "Why don't you get cleaned up? I'll hit my mom's closet for some clothes. You can at least start out mud-free before we take off again."

His breath moved tendrils of hair across her face. It tickled her skin, but she wasn't about to move from his arms. She needed to feel connected to someone, anyone, but was grateful it was Steve.

"What's going to happen?" She tried to remain calm, to keep the shakiness from her voice. "If they have the money *and* the formula, why not give Rory back?"

"I don't know, Janie. I really don't know."

"WE HAD...LEAD...OPERATIONS...moved...San Antonio."

"I'm only getting every other word, George." He was soaked to the skin after standing on the covered porch, but it was the only place his phone halfway worked. Steve glanced through the window to an empty living room as he spoke into his cell. "Can you hear me? She's innocent."

"I can have a team...evacuation point...approximately two hours...local PD to pick her up." George's distorted voice punched through the static on the connection.

"No." He hated the thought of Jane in handcuffs. "George, trust me. I don't need any help to get her to San Antonio. Set up around the Alamo like I asked so we can catch these bastards."

"You...way over your head. You know...and McCaffrey hit the roof...you were gone."

"I'm losing the connection, man. We'll meet you in San Antonio. Give me your word."

"You're wrong. You can't trust..."

"Just check it out for me."

"You...the river has crested...evacuated your area."

Beep. Beep. Beep.

"Son of a..." He resisted the impulse to throw the state-of-the-art piece of crap into the soggy yard. Before his broken phone call the lake had been a couple of feet from the house. Now it was creeping into his mother's flowers.

The homes on the north shore of Lake Buchanan had been evacuated since yesterday. Even though the lake was flood-regulated, it didn't stop the creeks that fed it from becoming dangerous flash-flood zones. The river had already crested and the rain kept coming down in sheets.

They'd lost time talking about the kidnapping. His job of helping victimized children had suddenly become grimly personal. The lake water rushed by, but he couldn't seem to get moving. He had one of those feelings of dread stuck in the pit of his stomach. He just couldn't pinpoint what Jane was lying about and the whole scenario of her son's kidnapping made no sense.

He was blown away. Jane had a kid. He shook his head, trying to keep his thoughts on track. They needed to leave.

Now. Steve had driven around the barricades to get to the house so they could use his rental to get back out.

Heeding his sense of urgency, he walked back into the house and straight to his mother's workroom. Straight into a table with his mother's scrapbook junk that he knocked to the floor. Crap. He knelt to pick up the pictures scattered on the carpet.

Baseball. First grade. Bobby Joe Hill.

Big as day, there was his friend with his arm around Steve's shoulder and two teeth missing.

The fear and confusion from that summer slammed his body, forcing its way into his mind. Shutting him down to hear his breathing echoing in his head.

If he hadn't thought he'd done the right thing by calling George, his memories confirmed his actions. Bobby Joe had disappeared without a trace. That wasn't going to happen to Jane's son.

He slammed the picture on the table, got a sweat suit and T-shirt from the back of the closet and left it on the bed in the guest room. Opening the bathroom door a crack, he said, "I've left some of Mom's clothes here. We need to head out."

"I'll be right there."

"The Colorado is already out of its banks. It's sure to cause problems and detours on the way to San Antonio."

The water cut off. He quickly pulled the door closed. No matter how much he wanted to be close to Jane, missing the kidnapper's deadline wasn't an option. He rubbed his aching head and found aspirin in the kitchen cabinet. He tossed back two tablets and half a can of soda.

A muffled thump had him reaching for his weapon—that was in his pack.

A couple of sporadic whacks outside got louder as he approached the mudroom and opened the door. The water covered the road leading to the driveway. He yanked his boots from his feet and let the door slam behind him.

JANE SEARCHED THE UNFAMILIAR room for a clock and confirmed she'd been in the shower less than ten minutes. She never should have let him convince her to clean up, but getting the filth off her skin helped regain control of her thoughts.

Loud thunder rumbled through the house as she pulled Amanda's sweats around her waist. Her feet tangled in the long pants, slowing her progress as she vaulted from the bed toward the window. Another strange thudding outside along with a string of colorful curses carried through the storm. Water lapped at the base of the porch. Steve's rental car floated in the flooded driveway, bumping into the sides of the detached garage.

There wasn't any way to get back to her rental which had probably washed away, too.

They'd lost their transportation, but couldn't wait around for rescue workers to get to them. She *had* to be in San Antonio ready to get Rory back tomorrow. Pulling the drawstring around her waist tighter, she ran down the stairs and pulled the porch door open just as Steve dove off the dock.

The downpour drenched her in a matter of seconds. The sky was dark and menacing. It was hard to see even though it was nine-fifteen in the morning.

They had another six or seven feet before the water would reach the first floor. But the contents from the garage—level with the lake—joined the rest of the flotsam.

Debris, trash, beach toys, a foam cooler and lots of tree limbs made it not only disgusting but very dangerous to swim through.

"Steve!" Was he crazy?

Then she saw the rope tied to the corner post of the porch. Her heart slowed just a bit from its rapid beat. With her eyes, she followed the rope toward the floating boat dock and prayed Steve had enough sense to tie the other end around himself.

"Steve!"

"I'm okay, Jane." He waved and swam farther away. He *was* crazy. "Wait there."

Another lightning flash, with an almost immediate crack of thunder, helped enough with the horrible visibility to see Steve swimming back with a Jet Ski in tow. Jane went to the rope and pulled the loose end from the water, tossing it to him when he got close.

"Grab my pack and shove my boots inside," he shouted through the rain. "They're in the laundry."

She should let him have a piece of her mind for scaring her half to death, but she didn't argue. She ran through the house and found his boots, shoving one worn shoe inside the bag, but something prevented the other from fitting. Rearranging things, she jumped when her hand connected with the cold metal of Steve's gun handle.

Calm down. He's FBI. He wouldn't go anywhere without this thing. Shoving the second boot inside, she tugged the too-big sweatpants up as she ran back to the porch.

Steve finished a couple of hitches around a post and turned his back on the Jet Ski. "Okay, I'm ready."

"So am I."

"Oh, no, you're not," he shouted sternly, placing his fists on his hips. "You're staying here."

"This is our only way out."

"It's too dangerous. I couldn't get to the life vests. The rain's coming down so hard I can't see twenty feet in front of me. The evacuation point will have rescue boats. I'll come back for you after I've gotten across to the south side."

"No." She shook her head, running a hand across her eyes only to have the rain replace the water as fast as she'd removed it. "We go together."

"Don't be so dang stubborn." Creases between his eyes emphasized how much he believed he was right.

"Me?" All the fright she'd experienced in the past three days surfaced faster than she could control. Words tumbled from her heart that she'd wanted to say for over four years. "You are the biggest, most stubborn, hardheaded, jackass of a man I've ever met."

"Oh, yeah? This Jet Ski is twelve years old. This hard head of mine might just survive getting across ten miles of lake on my own. The seat might just be big enough for my stubborn ass, but there's no way two of us can make it in this weather. Shoot, it's probably going to run out of gas anyway."

"You can't leave me behind."

"Yes, I can. It's too dangerous to take you with me. Now hand over my pack."

Although she'd experienced it only once, Jane knew that tough look he threw her way. He'd used the same one when he'd told her she couldn't pass up the opportunity to work for Johns Hopkins. But she wouldn't let him make decisions for her.

Not again.

Never taking her eyes from Steve's, she slipped one arm through a strap, then the other.

"Aw, hell," he moaned as lightning splintered across the sky. The storm wasn't backing off. It was getting worse. He stomped barefoot across the porch and angrily grabbed her shoulders. "You aren't a strong enough swimmer for this, Jane. No one's a strong enough swimmer for this."

"I'm going. Rory's depending on me." Stubborn? He only thought he'd seen stubborn before. Jutting her chin out, she gritted her teeth and prepared to fight him if necessary. *He* could stay here. *She'd* take the Jet Ski. Her mind raced to the self-defense book she'd read once.

Pictures flooded her mind. Steve's tall lanky frame would topple if she had the right move, but she didn't want to hurt him on the slick porch.

Then he freed her, pushed his hair out of his eyes and released a long sigh. "Get on."

Not waiting for a second invitation, she grabbed the sweatpants around her waist, inching the material from under her feet, then carefully walked the steps leading to the rising water and Jet Ski. She waited as Steve untied the rope from the post, wrapped some around his hand and followed her.

Standing on the slope with the lake rising around their calves, Steve tipped her chin to face him. The wind whipped the rain in stinging pelts against her skin, but she could barely feel it after his warm touch.

He wrapped and knotted the end of the rope around her waist. "I won't lose you, Janie."

His lips brushed hers firmly and much too briefly to be considered exciting. Yet all the euphoric sensations she'd experienced four years ago rushed back, making her light-headed.

Maybe it was just a lack of sleep.

The other end of the rope now hung around his waist. He waited for her to climb on, then led the Jet Ski away from the house.

With the rain assailing their bodies, Steve shoved them farther from shore, mumbling about her hardheadedness all the while. Then he pulled himself onto the ski and turned the starter.

"I wish I'd been more stubborn and kept you from pushing me away four years ago," she whispered softly into the back of his shirt.

He couldn't have heard her. The roar of the Jet Ski coming to life combined with the thunder and water crashing the muck against the porch drowned her whisper. But his hand squeezed her thigh and pulled her closer to him on the seat. He drew her arms tighter around his broad chest before he gunned the gas and headed into the gray, murky horizon.

Tell him.

The nagging voice kept pestering her to tell Steve he was Rory's father. But how? It wasn't possible on the back of a Jet Ski. She'd missed the opportunity to calmly inform him. He already thought she was half-crazy and would never believe she was telling the truth.

Jane had no choice but to trust that he'd help. She had to get to San Antonio and find Rory. Then she'd worry about telling Steve everything she should have a long time ago.

TRAVELING THROUGH A thunderstorm that could be classified as a mild monsoon and getting to safety should have been the most important things on Steve's mind. Well, they *were* priorities. Along with dodging the debris swept downstream by the Colorado River. He jerked the Jet Ski around another bobbing tree limb as thick as his thigh.

But Jane hung right there at the top of his problems. She hadn't moved an inch, still hugging his waist as tight as when they'd started out. He wanted to reassure her.

Better to just concentrate on getting across the lake.

It would be safer to stay near shore, but that wasn't an option. Too much debris, too much shoreline, too little gas. He knew of one possible evacuation site—the dam on the southwestern point of a hundred miles of shoreline. It was the only place people were still likely to be, and high enough that cars could still get to the roads.

It might as well have been pitch-dark for all the visibility he had, so he crept along like an old hound dog hunting for a scent. With no windshield on the Jet Ski, not even fools took these machines out in a mild rain. Especially with no life vests. The dang things had floated away before he could get to the boathouse.

Jane should have stayed at his parents' home where she'd be safe. But he couldn't risk making a mistake that might cost them finding her son. She would never forgive him.

He could beat himself up all day. It wouldn't do any good. They'd find Rory, the Brant kid and the money. He spied an unidentifiable floating object ahead and released the throttle.

"What's wrong?" Jane asked, shouting into the wind.

"Nothing. We're fine." They bumped into a lounge chair cushion and Steve pushed it away with his foot. He wiped the water from his face using the tail of his wet T-shirt and flexed his stiff fingers several times. "You doing okay?"

"How far do you think we've come?"

"A couple of miles."

"I'm glad you can make out where we're going. I can't see a thing."

Little did she know he couldn't see anything, either. He steered as best he could, keeping the cascade over his right shoulder. If the wind direction and slant of the rain were consistent, he just might manage to get them to the other end of the lake.

There wasn't much room on the seat. Reaching behind him with one hand, he scooted Jane's hips closer to his own. Half of him was glad for the close contact. The same half that loved the crazy *thump-thump-thump* his heart made whenever they were together. The other half kicked himself for letting her come along.

"Ready?" he asked, leaning forward to grab the throttle again.

"Yeah."

Jane's arms tightened once more, and she placed her face against his shirt. Back in his life a few hours, she made him feel more alive with one casual touch than any rush his current life provided.

Steve braced himself. He couldn't turn and avoid an impact with the object in front of him. The Jet Ski rammed into a log and the side of his head slammed into the handle. He lost his grip and flew off the seat.

Water rushed up to meet him. He lost all sense of direction and inhaled a gallon of water as he sank deeper each second.

Some long-forgotten training finally clicked on in his subconscious. He fought the impulse to save all his air and let some go, watching the bubbles rise. He kicked his legs hard and struggled back to precious air on the surface. A weight pulled at his midsection, making it more difficult to stay above the water.

He had to hurry and began to pull himself through the rough waves. He couldn't lose the Jet Ski several yards away.

His eyes stung from the water and the rain made it more

difficult to see. He could breathe again, but just barely with whatever was jerking him down.

God, the weight was Jane.

Chapter Four

Jane crashed through the surface and sucked air into her lungs, thankful she hadn't been thrown too deep. It was difficult to tread water with the baggy pants and heavy backpack pulling her down. Then a yank around her waist brought her head underwater again. Her breath turned to a choking terror until she broke the surface a second time.

"Jane!"

"I'm…fine…" She coughed. "Stop pulling. I'm… You're going to drown me." She tugged at the drawstring and kicked free of the sweatpants, making it much easier to stay above water.

"Thank God. You scared the crap out of me." He let the rope go slack. "We've gotta catch the ski."

"Go on, I'm right behind you."

Steve's pack made her movement through the water awkward, slowing her progress through the choppy waves. She barely had the strength to keep the rope slack between her and Steve.

He caught the Jet Ski and pulled himself precariously onto the seat. Getting behind him required balancing worthy of any high-wire act she'd seen. She rested her head on his shoulder and he reached behind her, pulling her tight against him. He kept one of her hands anchored around his waist while he steadied the Jet Ski in the waves and wind.

The surprise of hitting the water still had her breathing

hard. It had absolutely nothing to do with the lingering effect of Steve's hands on her backside or the reassuring squeeze his fingers had given her hand.

"Lucky we weren't going faster. We might have been in serious trouble," she said.

"You don't think of *this* as serious trouble?" he asked, wheezing on a deep breath, looking as exhausted as her body told her she was.

"I'm attempting to look on the bright side of things."

"And that is?"

"We're not unconscious or drowning." She coughed to clear more water from her lungs. "And we didn't lose our only way of getting across this lake faster than the backstroke."

His easy laughter was music to her heart. It made her want to forget everything that had happened and laugh, too. She loved having a reason to be squished next to him. To experience the thrill of their bodies close together like she imagined so often.

"What happened?" she asked to distract herself from thoughts about Steve.

"A very large tree limb. I've been dodging them. But this one got by me." He wrung out the corner of his shirt and lifted it to his face, coughing for several seconds.

"Are you okay?" she asked and pounded on his back.

"As soon as you stop beating me to death."

"Sorry. I didn't mean to—"

"I'm all right. I was just kidding."

He hadn't sounded as if he was kidding. Her judgment of people didn't have a great track record though. The book definition of *sarcasm* was locked in her brain, but she admitted her application needed improvement.

Steve put the key in the ignition and pushed the start button, but it didn't seem to have any effect. Even with the storm pounding and thunder reverberating through the air, the excruciating silence of the engine dropped a black curtain. All her hopes died.

"Come on, baby," Steve coaxed.

Then, with a couple of sputters the engine sprang to life, letting Jane breathe again. Her arms encircled Steve's body, probably clinging too tightly in her relief, but she didn't care. Her chest flattened against the ripcord muscles in his back, his labored breathing a comfort to her frayed nerves.

Even with the Jet Ski going as slowly as the throttle allowed, it was still horribly noisy for conversation. And what would she say? Steve couldn't afford to be distracted. As evidenced by their incident with the tree limb.

For the second time in an hour, the thought of losing Steve crossed her mind. First his crazy dive off the dock, now this. She forced herself to remember that he wasn't hers to lose. That had happened almost four years ago.

Their relationship had been intense from the start. A casual glance one moment and a flirtatious conversation the next. She rarely dated. She never had time.

Then or now.

But while awaiting word from research facilities and with the last of her classes finished, she couldn't tell Steve no. She'd turned off every control button programmed to keep her in check and threw caution to the wind.

They'd seen each other every day and every night for six weeks. Then Johns Hopkins called and he'd gone into full retreat. Of course, she hadn't realized the extent of his withdrawal at the time.

She'd analyzed his every move over the past four years. Comparing him to many case studies in the volumes of psychology books stored in her head. Steve Woods couldn't depend on anyone but himself. On the surface he appeared to be a guy not ready for a commitment.

More than once she had hoped there was something else. Something he hadn't shared with her. A deep dark secret that would explain why he'd pushed her aside. It didn't seem that way.

She'd grown to accept the rejection of herself, but she

couldn't snuff a spark of hope for Rory. Her son needed stability and roots. She'd moved back to Dallas to be closer to Steve and his family. In case anything happened to her, family was an anchor Rory needed. And Steve had plenty of family. She wanted to be settled, then introduce his son.

Right now she needed his help to find Rory without distractions—without the truth. After they found their son, she'd tell him everything and then they could determine what to do. She and Rory had managed without him once. If that was what he chose, they'd do it again.

The going was slow, even slower than before. She hadn't thought it possible to be this cold in July, but the northern rain kept beating down on them, chilling her inside and out with each painstaking minute of progression.

It stung her cheeks and exposed skin. So she buried her face between her arm and Steve's back. She didn't know how he managed to see where they were headed.

To take her mind off everything, she drew *The Missing Years of Merlin* from a shelf in her memory and skipped through the pages to her favorite scene. She'd recited parts of this story to Rory. He seemed to enjoy the words—or the excitement in her voice.

God, please keep him safe.

She couldn't think about him kidnapped, afraid, perhaps hurt. She wanted to remember holding him, fluffing his soft downy hair and kissing the side of his neck to hear his laughter. But it hurt too much. So she continued to read, hold on tight to Steve's waist and take comfort in his warmth.

"WAHOO!" STEVE THREW HIS head around, his laughter full of relief. "There it is, Janie. There's the LCRA."

"Wonderful." She ventured to peek around Steve's right to see where they were going.

Still thirty or so yards from the buoys, she couldn't distinguish figures. But one image leaped out. A policeman in a bright yellow slicker stood near his car while the red and blue lights turned in a silent warning.

"We can't go there, Steve. Turn around. Please." She tugged on his shirt and he released the throttle so the ski would idle in the water.

He turned to her with a questioning look. He must've thought she was crazy. Well, she thought that about herself regarding this entire ordeal. With every development she wanted to wake up and find it was all a horrible nightmare.

Each wave carried them closer, but no one seemed to have noticed yet.

"If you don't want to go to the shore, Jane, where do you suggest we go?"

"I can't walk up to a police officer and ask for help. Can't we go somewhere else and walk to the road?"

"Walk? Make our way through the swamp that's become the lakeshore? Barefoot through the cactus and God only knows what else? Just so we can get back to the very place we can see a few yards away?"

His voice rose with every ridiculous question, turning his deep baritone into an angry tenor. The tension sang through his body, transferring to Jane's hands at his waist. She let go, but his stress continued to zing through the air, as apparent as the lightning still above their heads.

"I can't take a chance on being incarcerated." She began untying the safety rope.

"Oh, no, you don't," Steve said as he stilled her fingers with his own. "You aren't swimming to shore alone. Why don't you trust me, Jane?"

"I can't." Emotion like she'd never experienced with another person crossed his face. Anger, hurt, confusion. They were all there and she was causing his pain. "I mean, I want to, but..."

"Yeah?"

"When it comes to the law, that's the only thing I *can* trust about you." He would always uphold the law. Always. The single most important thing to him was the law. Caring for her fell far beneath that craving he had to do the right thing. The doubts charged through her mind like the storm surrounding them.

Steve managed to turn enough to cup her soggy shoulder. She wanted to relax into him as his warmth shot all the way to her numb toes.

"I'm not going to let anyone take you. Your son is depending on us. Trust me." Lightning splintered the sky, giving an ominous feel to his words.

"I want to."

"Then do it." His voice rose above the thunder. "Don't analyze it to death, just do it. Isn't there a book somewhere in there—" his eyes darted to her forehead "—that supports taking a chance on me?"

He faced front again and gunned the gas, not giving her an opportunity to make up her mind.

They shot forward, and she grabbed the sides of Steve's shirt. A man in a bright orange slicker waited at the edge of the dock and tossed a rope to Steve. Then he offered her a hand. His sturdiness kept her from sliding into the lake as she gained the use of her jellylike legs and untied the rope around her waist. She tugged at the sweatshirt, finally glad it was too big, and covered her bottom better than her bikini underwear.

"Looks like you folks had a rough time of it," he said. He was a weathered man of at least sixty-five, but had strength in his thick hands. "Just about everybody left yesterday."

After securing the Jet Ski—something she had no desire to ever ride again—Steve stuck out his hand to the old guy.

"Brandon Woods. This is my wife, Mary Beth. We were checking on my parents' house on the northwest shore. Things seemed to have escalated faster than we anticipated."

Brandon and Mary Beth…his brother and sister-in-law.

"Can't ever turn your back on the water, can you? I'm Cap Harvey. Pleased to meet you both." He captured her hand between his again, never lowering his eyes to her exposed legs. "I'd offer you some coffee, but I'm a figurin' you'll want out of here as soon as possible. You're just in time to catch the last transportation leaving for the Llano High School gymnasium."

The police officer got into his car, but didn't pull away.

"The evacuation center is set up there, and they'll take care of you. Ain't a pretty ride, but it'll get you out of here." Cap pointed to a dented, rusty panel van on the other side of the cop car. "Plenty of hot coffee to warm your chilled bones in the gym. Yes, sir. Now, let's pull this ski 'round to the side and secure it. I'll need to lock up and we'll be on our way."

Jane attempted to blend into the background. Shocked, she could barely manage a thought. Steve had lied for her, claiming to be his brother. Had he changed his mind about contacting the FBI?

"Will it be okay to leave the ski here till things settle down?" Steve asked. "My dad will be around as soon as folks are allowed back in."

"Can't make no guarantees, but no one ever can. That young wife of yours looks like she's gonna turn blue with her next breath. You'd best get her out of this downpour. There's a dry blanket in the van."

"Mary Beth?" Steve shook her shoulder. "Come on, sweetheart. You need to get dry."

"Thank you," she said as she passed Cap.

Her *husband*—how many times had she wished that were true?—draped his arm around her shoulders and tucked her next to his soggy T-shirt. The rain still fell hard and Jane blinked away drops that clung to her eyelashes while they walked to the empty van.

No seats except up front. Most of the space was jam-packed with animals secured in cages of all shapes and sizes, including the passenger side. They made their way to the back door. The overpowering smell of wet fur and other wet substances she didn't want to name aloud besieged her nose.

Steve spoke through a crack in the door. "I'll be right back."

The door slammed.

The rain pounded on the roof.

A cockatiel squawked. "Dasypus novemcinctus."

A nine-banded Armadillo made a soft snorting noise. "Nymphicus hollandicus."

A cat hissed. "Felis silvestris catus. More commonly referred to as felis catus. One of four subspecies of felis silvestris."

Listing the scientific name of each caged animal passed the time and kept her mind from straying to thoughts of Rory, kidnappers, police or Steve. But that was exactly what she was thinking about: Rory, kidnappers, police *and* Steve.

Life in Baltimore had been lonely, but not frightening. At least not after Rory arrived. She could handle being alone. It was the thought of being totally responsible for a miniature Steve that had her lying awake at night. Wondering if she would screw up her child as much as her parents had emotionally handicapped her.

Having her late in their lives, they'd retired and moved closer to each school they felt would give a child genius the best education. Or the most collegiate exposure. They had provided her a safe life without friends. Complicated, exploited, full of their version of love.

And secretive. She learned early in life not to let others know she had nearly one hundred percent recall. It scared some people to be around her. Others didn't want her to outshine them with her knowledge. It intimated every boy she'd ever had a crush on.

Resulting in a life of holding back. Answering only the questions asked.

Oh, she'd done all the analysis. She knew all the correct terms and what she should do to "feel better." She had been satisfied with her life until Steve had shown her something more. Rory was a blessing, a wake-up call that there was more to life than research and new discoveries.

The pregnancy had been frightening until her son had actually arrived. When she'd heard his cry, counted his fingers and toes, then she'd rested easy. Maybe Steve was ready to change? Maybe he could get things straightened out and find their son. She had to tell him the truth.

The wind pushed at the van, slapping the drops of rain against the windshield. Through the downpour she could see Steve's outline leaning against the window of the police car.

Unfamiliar panic bubbled in her throat. She wanted to scream like a crazy woman. He was turning her in. It had all been a trick to get her to let her guard down. What could she do?

What would happen to Rory?

She searched the van for some type of defense. Nothing. Just cages, blankets and more cages. She couldn't let Rory down. She glanced at Steve, still with the cop. If she could make the tree line she'd find another way to the rendezvous.

Jane grabbed Steve's pack, searching for cash. She rummaged until she fingered his gun. She would get to San Antonio.

Any way she had to.

Wait. Breathe. Get control. The calming exercises she practiced daily kicked in. She could think anything through to its logical conclusion. Methodically. Steve wouldn't have put her in this metal menagerie if he wanted the police to take her away. He could have easily overpowered her and delivered her to the cops.

Cap got in the van and shook the water from his hair. "You folks just barely caught me. We'll be the last car through on 29 before they shut her down."

He honked and got Steve's attention. Her pretend husband waved to the cop and ran back to the van. The door slammed behind him, and he sat next to her at the rear of the cargo, which was the only free space available among the strange assortment of animals. He wrapped a blanket around his shoulders, rubbed the water from his face and stared at her.

Did she look guilty? Look as though she'd stolen money and had her hand on a gun under the blanket?

"Can't believe it's eleven in the morning. Practically dark outside," Cap said from the front seat. "Hope you don't mind, but we've got one more rescue to make before I can get you to the Red Cross. Old Mrs. Walters couldn't get back to get her pet Genevieve. She's the next house up the road. After that, Llano's 'bout twenty miles, but in this rain, it'll seem more like forty."

Steve didn't answer. Cap droned on, and Jane stopped hearing his words. Thoughts of possible scenarios involving Rory's abductors spun through her mind, making it difficult to think of anything else.

The noise level in the van tripled when they began moving. The potholed dirt road they followed to pick up Genevieve created lots of noise and unrest among the animals. And each bump sent a small wave of musty odors Jane's direction until she covered her nose with the blanket. But the results weren't much better, since the damp cover had been in the muggy van a while.

Steve put his arm around her, but she pulled away. She'd rather get a knot on her head from bumping against the side of the van than be unable to concentrate.

The van stopped. "This won't take but a minute. You two try to keep warm."

"We need to talk," Steve said as soon as the door closed.

His brows were drawn together in thought. His dark eyes made darker because of the low light and his longish hair drying close to his head caused him to look much younger than his thirty-two years. She pushed his looks aside and concentrated on his words.

"Won't I just have to repeat everything to the cops or will your FBI friends be waiting at the Red Cross center?"

"What?"

"You told that police officer—"

"I asked the sheriff about transportation to San Antonio and what the roads were like."

She gulped back the rest of her accusation. "You did?"

"Yes, I did."

Steve watched the shadows lift from her eyes with, what, hope? He deliberately knocked his head on the panel behind him. What was another lump on his tough skull?

Doesn't she know she can trust me with her life? He wouldn't just hand her to a cop.

But what about the phone call to George? There was a logical reason for that. His team needed the information that Jane supplied in order to find the kidnappers.

So why not tell her about it? He should. But would she understand? They couldn't go to San Antonio blind. They needed control of the situation. They could only gain that through his team. He wouldn't feel guilty for doing his job.

"Why didn't you call me, Steve?"

Because wanting to scared me to death.

He couldn't tell her that. Not in the back of a panel van surrounded by wet, stinky animals. Not with her son missing. Not without his arms around her.

Every unspoken word caused the rift between them to widen. She drew her knees close to her chest, visibly withdrawing further from him. He wanted to explain, but the words caught in his throat.

"Never mind. It doesn't matter," she said.

"Of course it matters."

As they raised their voices, so did the tension among the animals. They circled or squirmed in their cages, causing all kinds of racket. Just like the dive-bombing butterflies in Steve's stomach. He swallowed hard.

It didn't matter where they were. Just like his grandpop always said, "Saddle up, cowboy, time to ride." Now he knew what that meant.

The back door flew open. Steve's floundering for the right words stopped when Cap handed him a heavy sack.

"Don't have any more cages, and Genevieve's glass was just too heavy to move. Mind keeping a hold on her?" Cap asked.

He didn't give Steve a chance to answer, just slammed the door and got in the front, humming. Jane's eyes opened wide and she shrugged.

"Don't sneak a peek at her now," Cap said. "She's a little upset."

Holding the dingy slithering bag as far away from his body as possible, Steve asked, "What kind of snake is she?"

"Baby python."

"Great." Steve swallowed the lump in his throat. He'd wanted something to occupy his hands, but this went too far.

From the reaction of the other animals, they didn't care much for the idea of traveling with the reptile, either. Between their restlessness, the pounding rain and just the general road noise of a metal van, it was nearly impossible to hold any type of discussion. Let alone a private one.

"I'll hold it if you'd like," Jane raised her voice to say. "I remember how much you hate snakes."

"It's okay as long as it stays in the sack."

A light airy laugh filled his ears, but didn't last long enough. Amusement was soon replaced by a look of forlorn longing. He recognized it easily enough. The look of a mother wondering where her child was. The look of a parent who realized they might never see their child again.

Damn the criminals for involving Jane and her son.

Damn them for doing this to anyone.

"SOMETHIN' MUST HAVE happened to somebody important," the driver shouted over the animals. "There's a chopper in the middle of the baseball field."

Steve shot up to his knees, rocking back and forth with the motion of the van as they turned into the school's dirt parking lot. White-hot anger shot through him like a speeding bullet. "Son of a… I told them not to come!"

"What? You're turning me in?"

Her hurt sliced through him. He saw every millisecond of his world—the possible world with Jane and Rory—falling apart.

Steve's mouth went dry. He reached for her, but she pulled the blanket tighter around her shoulders.

As if in slow motion, George, McCaffrey and Stubblefield rushed from the building with guns drawn. The sheriff had obviously notified them that they were in this van.

The doors slowly opened. The rain drizzled inside at his knees. His hands automatically went above his head, one still holding the sack containing Genevieve. The blanket fell away from one of Jane's shoulders, and he caught sight of the black canvas of his pack.

Unzipped. His boots lay on the metal floor next to it.

The barrel of his gun pointed toward his coworkers.

No way. She had to be bluffing. He had to stop things before they got more out of hand.

Jane couldn't pull the trigger. He knew that. Right? But his team didn't know. Had they seen the gun yet? No, it was still blocked from their view by the blanket. Jane was desperate. She couldn't know what she was doing.

Genevieve the snake fell to the top of the armadillo's cage as Steve pretended to slip on the wet floor. He aimed his body for Jane's lap and the gun. She tried to move out of his way, and they dropped into the muddy parking lot.

As they fell, he searched Jane's eyes, seeing the surprise and betrayal.

"Don't pull the trigger, Jane."

Chapter Five

Rope and hog-tie someone. That was what Steve would do to the next person through that door. If he had his .45, he just might shoot them. Lucky for him they'd taken it as evidence before bringing him to the San Antonio FBI building.

While he'd been shuffled from one room to another being debriefed, his FBI comrades had managed three rounds of interrogation with Jane. They'd been picked up eight hours ago and had been drilling her hard. The last round led by his partner and friend, George Lanning.

Stuck alone in this observation room for the past forty-seven minutes, he knew every inch of the monitor in the corner. The black-and-white image of Jane was burned into his memory. He'd never forget.

And she'd never forgive.

One delicate hand propped up her chin. The other was cuffed to a metal ring, keeping her from moving around the room. It was absurd to actually think she might attack one of the two-hundred-pound men in there with her.

George rapidly fired off question after question. Steve knew the drill. Try to trip up the suspect. Make it hard to keep up with the individual items being asked. Attempt to get the real, unplanned answers by not allowing time for thought.

As fast as events had happened in the past twenty-four hours, Jane should have been physically exhausted and emotionally empty. But she calmly and methodically answered each question presented. She only broke eye contact when George wouldn't answer whether she would be allowed to meet the kidnappers in the morning.

Each time her story had been the same—a frustrating tale of events that were incredible, but true. They were back at the beginning.

The door behind Steve opened. He turned to see a white tissue waving through the crack. George entered, staying close to the door. Steve smirked. "You really think I'll launch myself across the room at you?"

"Wouldn't put it past you."

Good. He should understand that he was pissed at him. George was the only person who could have informed the team where to pick Jane up. Why hadn't he trusted Steve?

"At least uncuff her." He slammed his palm against the wall, causing a faded watercolor as old as the building to tilt lopsided near George. How could he help Jane? He felt as guilty as original sin and as helpless as a newborn colt.

"Get a grip, man. You're so close to this, you aren't thinking straight." His partner leveled the frame. "Proven by the fact that you withheld information, that you—"

"Jane's son has been kidnapped." Somehow his mouth didn't trip over the words. "Jane is… God, George, what are you guys doing to her? Why hasn't she at least been allowed to clean up? At least give her some pants."

Mud still clung to her T-shirt from their fall in the dirt lot. Her hair had dried in the ringlets she hated, making her look young and innocent. She was innocent. And naive. His gut wrenched.

This was all his fault. He shouldn't have contacted the Bureau. He should have listened to Jane.

"It isn't my call, Steve," George answered, turning away and avoiding eye contact.

If Steve gritted his teeth any harder, he'd break a tooth. "Where's McCaffrey?"

"That's Special Agent McCaffrey to you, Woods." The

door clicked shut behind the older agent who stood rigid in his customary black suit reeking of Old Spice.

"Why is Jane still cuffed? She's not a suspect. Haven't you heard a word of her explanation?" He was tired of waiting and wanted answers. Now. "This case doesn't fit any of the profiles. Whatever you believe, Jane is the key. I need to stick by her like glue. That's the only way to get Rory and the Brant kid back."

"Have a seat, Woods."

Steve glanced again at the screen. Jane must be as frustrated as he was at the lack of information. Her head rested on her free arm, her face hidden from the camera. How would he ever make this right with her?

They hadn't been allowed to talk. He'd been cooped up with agent after agent, but no one would tell him anything. A red-hot resentment seeped through him. George. His partner. His Judas.

He'd never forgive himself if something happened to Jane or her son because of his obligatory sense of duty to report in. His anger toward George for letting McCaffrey know where they were going tore at his gut. If he experienced this toward his partner, how deep was the betrayal Jane suffered toward him?

He took a deep breath and tried a calmer voice. "Why is she still cuffed?"

"We take threatening federal agents with a deadly weapon very seriously around here." McCaffrey shrugged and placed a manila folder on a side table.

"I told you. My gun, my fault." Steve shrugged and hoped the lie held water. "I slipped and it fell from the back of my jeans."

"And I replied I didn't believe you. Now sit down."

His voice was forceful, but Steve was ready to go over McCaffrey's head—or ready to take it off. He didn't care which.

"Sit down, buddy." George patted him on the shoulder and Steve stiffened.

He flipped a chair around and straddled the seat. It wasn't very professional, but he'd been relieved from duty. His partner continued to avoid eye contact. And the constant thorn in his side, Special Agent Roger McCaffrey, stood across the room tapping his fingers on his crossed arms.

"What's going on?" Steve asked.

Seconds crawled while George shifted uneasily and McCaffrey watched him like a spider ready to drop from his web.

At first he'd thought his team acted awkward because McCaffrey had taken over. It wasn't the first time Steve's methods had been questioned, and it wasn't the first time McCaffrey had relieved him of duty. They seemed to butt heads more often than a pair of randy rams.

But this was different.

"Would one of you just spill it?"

McCaffrey opened his mouth, but George shook his head. His partner paused and looked at the screen, bringing Steve's gaze back to it. Jane hadn't moved.

"We checked out Dr. Palmer's story. I'm sorry to have to tell you this, man, but Rory… Well, he died three months ago."

Shock was a word he thought he understood. Especially after the day he'd just lived.

Jane had a son.

Now she didn't?

What was the proper response to something like that? No. Jane wouldn't have lied. Something was wrong. Were they trying to run something on him? "Are…" He cleared the lump from his throat, playing their game. "Are you sure?"

"Yeah. Stubblefield ran it three times. Rory Palmer died from complications of pneumonia."

"It's a mistake." Steve scrubbed his face to hide his expression. For an instant, pain hit him hard. His eyes clouded so he covered them, pretending they ached, hiding the fact he wanted to rip someone's head off for suggesting this to him.

"The company shrink says it makes sense. You rescue kids, Steve," George explained. "She came to you with this problem. She might have arrived at a point where she couldn't separate reality from what she wanted to be true."

"You're wrong." God, did they really believe that psychobabble? Jane wasn't lying.

"She's been on antipsychotic drugs. There's no Mrs. Newinsky in her building. I'm sorry for her loss, but Palmer is our kidnapper." McCaffrey stood straight and looked smug, not sympathetic. "All we need now is the accomplice, Brant's location and the money. We think you can get that information for us."

"You're saying she's crazy?" Steve stood, knocking the chair to the floor in his haste. They better not be telling Jane any of this.

"We're stating facts," McCaffrey confirmed flatly, but took a step back.

"Facts? This is ridiculous. Jane isn't insane or delusional or any other crackpot name you want to call her. Just how she fits into all this bull I don't know, but I'm going to find out."

"Calm down, Woods," McCaffrey said.

"Does that look like a crazy person to you?" Steve pointed at the monitor, to a perfectly calm woman.

"Does that look like a mother frantic for her kidnapped son?" McCaffrey threw back at him. "Don't you think she'd be a bit more desperate if she didn't know where her kid was?"

Steve could only shake his head. "You don't know her. Jane isn't lying. Give her a poly."

"You're right, man." George finally looked directly at him. "We already did. She doesn't think she's lying. That's why the shrink said she passed."

"I'm ordering you to obtain the whereabouts of the Brant child." McCaffrey stood his ground, his face unchanging.

It was just another case to him. He didn't care if one of his agents was personally involved or not.

"You've been working abductions for a long time, Steve. Why would someone go to the trouble of forging a death certificate?" George asked.

"I don't believe it. Jane isn't a kidnapper." This case was one complicated circumstance after another. "Just have the locals in Baltimore verify her story."

George couldn't meet his eyes. "This is a mistake."

"Just talk to her, Steve," George prodded.

"What if I believe her?"

McCaffrey handed him the folder from the table, and George set the chair to rights. Steve flipped through the papers until he turned to the death certificate.

Time. He needed to think, analyze. Whoever was behind this was extremely thorough. But why? Why make it look like Jane was crazy?

One million individual reasons, he reminded himself. That was why it would be worth it to frame Jane and keep the FBI from looking somewhere else. At least long enough to get out of the country.

"There's a simple way to prove Jane's telling the truth. Interview her neighbors, coworkers at Johns Hopkins. Wait, she said that job didn't work out."

"Stubblefield's coordinating with the Baltimore police, but it's a holiday weekend." George's body language and attitude were the same Steve had when others questioned his capability.

"We can't wait any longer," McCaffrey said from somewhere behind Steve. "It's been two days and we need the location where the boy's being held. Now."

He had to find some way to function. Some way out of this.

Seconds ticked by on his watch. Somewhere it registered that they waited for an answer, but what could he say? He caught McCaffrey's impatient stance, the shifting of weight, the tapping of fingers on his expensive suit.

The unfeeling bastard.

"Uncuff her and get us some sodas."

"Good choice, Woods." McCaffrey held out his hand.

Steve gave him the folder, shrugging off the pat on the back the special agent in charge awkwardly gave. "I'm not doing this for you." He filtered the four-letter words he wanted to spew along with the look of *don't ever touch me again*.

"I don't care what your personal reasons are. Just get it done."

"No cameras, no recordings. What I have to say is private."

"Absolutely not," McCaffrey stated.

"Find the Brant kid on your own." Steve leaned back and tucked his shaking hands in his armpits. He would lose his job, but that wasn't why he was unsteady. If he didn't get back on this case, he might be throwing away his only chance to find Jane's son. Because he believed her.

"I could have your badge and lock you up for this."

"Yeah, but you won't. The publicity would endanger Thomas Brant." He felt stronger. "And believe me, I'll be a big pain in your media ass."

McCaffrey inclined his head to George, giving permission to leave and get things set up. "I won't forget this, Woods."

"Neither will I." He answered the special agent with just as much intimidation, but felt none of it. He was bluffing, but McCaffrey didn't know him well enough. Steve wouldn't endanger any child. He couldn't.

His soon-to-be ex-partner tossed a key to Steve. He folded his fist around the warm metal. At least he'd have her out of the cuffs. "While you're at it, McCaffrey, I'm off medical and back on the case. There's a few things we're going to have to do."

"Don't push it," McCaffrey said.

"We'll need to go through with the exchange in the morning.

If Jane is crazy…" Not in a million years. "We need to make her feel like we believe her story. Set up around the Alamo, track her and we'll find the Brant boy."

"It's too risky."

"It's our only shot." Steve stood his ground.

The answer to these strange events was there, buried just under the surface, waiting to be found. Because everything in him believed in Jane. Right or wrong, he'd made his decision. He would help her and find her son.

No matter what that meant.

JANE LOST TRACK OF THE number of hours she'd been sitting. Her legs cramped from the extra physical strain of the past two days. She longed to pace the worn tile. She'd never been arrested and didn't want to ever experience any part of it again. But if it guaranteed Rory's safety, she'd do anything.

Would the kidnappers deliver her son if she weren't at the Alamo like they'd instructed? She had to convince the FBI to let her participate. But how?

Maybe she should reconsider obtaining a lawyer. She searched her memory for a law book. Surely she'd read one? But nothing she recalled referred to federal kidnapping charges.

Where are you, Steve? She didn't want him to be her only hope, but it seemed that was the case.

Then she opened her eyes, and he stood in front of her. As if she'd conjured him from her fantasies, he bent to one knee and unlocked the handcuff.

"I didn't hear you come in." What an unintelligent thing to say. But her mind wouldn't work when his cool fingers gently rubbed her raw skin.

"You okay?"

Was that true concern in his voice? "Are you referring to how awful I must look, my wrist or the fact that Rory is still missing?"

"All of the above. Can we talk?"

Without waiting for an answer, he joined her at the table. The yellow notepad didn't escape her notice. She yearned for him to push the paper aside and hold her instead. But he was here to question her. Not to give comfort. She stood and took a shaky step back, away from the table and Steve. "When is the FBI going to believe I was blackmailed into helping with the second kidnapping?"

"I'm here to help."

"How? By asking me all the questions that I've already answered?" She rubbed her wrist and looked at Steve's clean clothes. She still smelled like the animals from the van. "I can't live with myself if anything happens to him. You've got to convince your team to let me meet the kidnappers in the morning and get him back."

"That's no longer a problem," he said softly. He stood again and followed her across the room. His expression was a bland mask, but his body was taut and alert. "You don't trust me?"

"Why should I?" She took another step away. Steve took another toward her, backing her into the corner. Just when her shoulders hit the wall and she couldn't retreat any farther, he abruptly turned and walked to the opposite side of the room. He calmly ripped the wire from the back of the camera mounted there. Returning to her, he managed to get his body even closer.

"Maybe because I want to get Rory back as much as you do? Didn't you find anything in here," he whispered and touched her forehead, "to support my side of things?"

Afraid that the closeness of his body had impaired her speech, she could only shake her head.

"How about here?" He touched her breastbone, just above her heart.

It was an innocent enough connection, but he was so close and leaning closer that it set her thoughts off balance. His warm breath caressed her ear, sending a tremor through her senses.

"If you didn't really trust me, why did you ask for my help, Janie?"

Janie. She'd always loved it when he called her that. She felt her knees weaken, then mentally shook herself to get her wits back. She tried to push him away, but his hands were firmly planted on either side, caging her in. His body didn't budge, as if he'd been prepared for her pathetic attempt at freedom.

"I shouldn't have asked, but I thought you would help find…" Dear Lord, she'd nearly said "your son." Her deliberate acidic tone still didn't get him to back up, although he momentarily averted his eyes.

His lips skimmed her neck, sending goose bumps over her flesh. She heard his deep breath and withstood the long, soft release across her sensitive skin. He smelled like soap. The direct opposite of the muddy picture she presented. His hair curled slightly above the collar of his T-shirt. The urge to hook her fingers through his belt loops fled only when he spoke.

"Before we can go forward, Janie…" He probably knew what that name did to her. "You've got to believe I'm the only person who can help you."

She pushed harder on his shoulders, but he managed to get closer and crowd her farther into the corner. "What are you doing?" she asked, glancing at the two-way mirror. "They're watching us."

"Probably. But the camera and tape aren't recording. I asked for some time alone with you." He swallowed hard and looked above their heads.

A little white box, similar to ones she'd seen on television shows, proved he'd maneuvered her out of sight of a second lens. His lowered voice indicated he didn't totally trust that no one was listening.

"If you had told me about Rory," he continued, his voice craggy and tired, "I would have come to you." Why did his heart race under her fingertips? Was his body actually shaking? "You've got to believe me, Jane."

He knows? Did he find out that Rory is his? Or...

"Oh, God, something's happened to Rory."

Steve's fingers held her wrists in place; she couldn't get free. She had to get out of here.

"We haven't had any word. Really."

"Then what's wrong?"

His lids hid his brown eyes for a moment before he leaned even closer to whisper in her ear. "We *will* find Rory. You have to trust me."

Despite every betrayal, every heartbreak and every frightening moment of the past four days, she did trust him. There was no logic to it. No solid reason she should, but she did.

"Why don't they believe me, Steve?"

Barely as a whisper, he spoke into her ear again. "Tomorrow, if something goes wrong..." His thumb caressed the inside of her wrist. Couldn't he just hold her? "You get to the Hilton Palacio del Rio. Wait for me in the Itazaba Lounge on the River."

True fear gripped her throat and squeezed.

"Do you understand me, Janie?"

"Yes." But she couldn't really think. She was so tired. Her knees almost buckled, causing Steve to hold her in place against the wall.

"Good. They'll be here any second. Try to hang on a while longer."

Mechanically, her body followed his instructions. For some reason, they believed she had something to do with the Brant kidnapping. Steve was warning and trying to protect her.

"You can't do this, Steve," she whispered while he led her to the chair. "If something happens, you need to find Rory. Forget about me."

"I...can't do that."

The door opened and Agent George Lanning ushered in

a female agent carrying a tray with drinks and sacks. Steve backed up, looking furious.

"Hey, man, I thought you'd want food with the sodas." He stayed close to the door, making eye contact with Steve. They exchanged an unspoken conversation she couldn't decipher. "Agent Branch is here to escort Dr. Palmer to clean up just as soon as she's eaten."

"What about McCaffrey?" Steve asked.

"*Special Agent* McCaffrey," he said, sounding exasperated, "agrees that Dr. Palmer should meet the kidnappers in the Plaza. We'll have operatives in place to make certain everything goes smoothly."

"Oh, thank God." Two days of tension evaporated. She wanted to cry, shout, sleep.

Steve had promised not to let anything happen to their son. She didn't care about anything else. She closed her eyes and blocked everyone in the small interrogation room from her mind. She needed her strength and concentration tomorrow.

Now she could rest.

Chapter Six

Alamo Plaza was filled with artisans and vendors. How was she ever going to find Rory in this crowd? Jane passed booth after booth of paintings, good and bad. Bronze and silver statues, homemade magnets, food… Everything blurred together like the agents' voices in her ear.

Shoppers passed, their bags brimming with specials from the temporary canvas stores. As they leisurely strolled by, she wondered if their glances were purposely casual or the eyes of Rory's kidnappers.

Her stomach tightened with the hope that this nightmare would soon be over. To have her son in her arms was all she'd dreamed about in the catnaps allotted her throughout the night.

Men and women talked back and forth across sophisticated wireless microphones and receivers. Through her FBI earpiece she heard them check in every four minutes now that it was ten past the hour.

The kidnapper was late.

Late…behind, delayed, held up, lagging, overdue, put off, slow, tardy. She ran through the list of synonyms to keep her mind off another couple of words…no show. *Don't go there,* she told herself. She had to keep it together.

The emotions fumed inside her faster than the San Antonio humidity. Storm clouds gathered ominously around the horizon, symbolic of trouble ahead, while sunshine beamed over her, leaving a ray of hope in its wake.

"Should I walk around?"

"Remember not to talk to yourself since you're probably being watched. Stay at the entrance, that's the best you can do," Steve said clearly in her inner ear. "Being late is completely normal. He's checking things out, seeing if he can finger any agents or cops."

His voice was gentle and soothed her frayed nerves whether he was lying or not. How could he maintain calm when their son might be... *Don't go there.* Steve was a professional. Several people around her were. And he still didn't know he was Rory's father.

Perhaps it was better this way. He could perform his duties and not be distracted by fatherly concern or contempt toward her.

The couple to her right, reading every name on the Alamo Cenotaph, she recognized from when she'd entered the FBI building yesterday. The older guy sitting on the bench, feeding the pigeons. He hadn't had the beard this morning when he'd brought her a cup of coffee. The guy with the camera and tripod. His name was George Lanning, and he'd questioned her about the kidnapping.

"Jane. Janie!" Steve's voice snapped her eyes toward the window where his team observed Alamo Plaza.

"Hmm?"

"Quit making our agents."

More nervous than before and afraid her mistakes would cost her son's life, she nervously covered her mouth. "What do you mean?"

"You're looking up at me now. Try to relax and act like a sightseer." He laughed, teasing or worried she had just shown the kidnappers where each agent was located.

"The note said to come by myself. Do you think he's not here because he's seen—"

"Stop, Jane. He'll show."

Such confidence. She yearned to share it, but this was all her fault. She had trusted the wrong person. Persons. First Mrs. Newinsky and then Steve. If the kidnappers didn't show because the FBI was here, it was completely her blunder. What would happen if they didn't find Rory? She'd shrivel and die inside.

A chill cooled her body despite the climbing heat of the southern Texas sun. She crossed her arms and rubbed her hands over her clammy skin.

"How much longer?" she asked through a tightly gripped jaw.

More tourists disembarked from a bus on the corner. The sidewalks were full of shoppers of every age. Children laughed and ran through the Plaza. She wanted to grab their parents and warn them of what could happen when they dropped their guard for just a moment.

"Don't lose it, sweetheart. You can do this."

Steve's voice seemed far-off. He was right. She *was* on the verge of losing it.

Breathe in. Breathe out. Take control of the emotion. Turn it into positive energy.

The deep breathing worked and she gained a clearer sense of awareness. Heat prickled the skin on her bare arms, irritating the raw skin around her right wrist. She tucked the plain new T-shirt farther into her jeans that thankfully weren't too tight around her waist. Some FBI person had shopped at an all-night Walmart to provide the new clothing. Even her tennis shoes weren't too bad a fit.

Steve had borrowed sunglasses from a slender brunette named Selena Stubblefield. The plastic frames slid lower on her nose as she caught sight of a Texas park ranger rounding the corner. Would the kidnapper avoid her because the ranger stood too near?

"Pardon me."

Jane whirled, making the apparent mother of three tow-headed boys all just below her elbow take a step back.

"Sorry, I was wondering if you could take our picture?"

The camera was thrust into Jane's hands before she could refuse. She moved closer to the street in order to get as much of the building in the snapshot as possible.

"I'm sorry, sir, but you'll have to remove the dogs to the other side of the street," the ranger said to a man in black with two yelping schnauzers.

The three boys chased each other into place around their mother's legs until she scolded them into being still. Each had matching burnt-orange shirts with a drawing of longhorns across their chests.

"I'm just going right there to the Menger Hotel," argued the dog guy.

"Smile," she told the family.

Click.

"Can you take another?" the woman asked. "Russell was making a face."

"Sure." Jane's eyes darted around the plaza.

"I'm sorry, sir. Dogs aren't allowed."

Click. Bark.

"Oh, thank you. It'll be the first picture of us all together." The woman took her camera. The boys punched each other in their arms.

The man with the schnauzers moved closer to the Alamo.

The park ranger grabbed the leashes.

People stopped to stare at the commotion.

It was all surreal. Jane stood on the edge of the crowd taking in the information, barely processing the events unfolding around her, unable to acknowledge the voices in her ear.

Don't you all know my son has been kidnapped! she yearned to scream.

A young girl tugged on her shirtsleeve and held up a folded piece of paper. Jane's hand extended.

"I'm supposed to give this to you." Then she skipped away.

Dogs barked. Men yelled. People in the crowd booed.

"George, flash your badge to the ranger and break up that crowd. Windstrom, stay on the girl," Steve's voice yelled in her ear. "Did anyone see where the note came from? Read it, Jane."

With trembling fingers she opened the message.

I should get rid of the boy since you didn't obey me.
You have one LAST chance.
Go inside and find the Tennessee flag.
ALONE.
Shove this paper in your pocket.
Ignore your new friends.

The kidnapper might "get rid" of Rory? Oh, God.

"I have to go inside. Alone." She crumbled the paper and put it in her pocket as instructed. "He knows you're here, Steve. Please stay away."

"Read it to me, Janie," he pleaded. "Team Two, cover the perimeter. I don't like this."

The urge to run overwhelmed her, but she held her legs back. And as much as she wanted Steve and his team to help, she knew she had to do this on her own.

Alone.

Just like the note said.

It took a few seconds for her eyes to adjust to the cool dark of the Alamo. Flags stood in every alcove. She scanned the signs and numbers indicating how many deaths each flag represented. Scotland, Rhode Island, Georgia, Kentucky, Minnesota—the names flew by as she searched for Tennessee.

Whispering from the crowd and the dim light added to the tension. Then just beyond the small rooms, a red flag stood alone. Tennessee. A white grocery sack lay on the floor, next to the stone wall and the flag's base.

"Jane, I just entered the building. Don't be surprised when you see me."

The kidnapper was sure to be watching her. She ignored Steve's voice and opened the sack, pulling out another note.

Shirt. Wig. Cap.
East entrance of the Alamo.
Menger Hotel, Message for RHONDA FRASER.

She ducked between the wall and two men talking about professional baseball. They turned toward the door and she slipped out of the building. Her heart beat triple time as she ran to the restrooms at the back wall and pulled the shirt and wig on.

"This is too dangerous, Jane. You can't do this on your own. Let me help," Steve said among the voices reporting in.

He hadn't seen her.

Throwing the sunglasses in the trash, she headed for the door and pulled on the black ball cap to just above her eyes. She was tempted to throw away the FBI earpiece, but it might prove better to know where the agents were and what they were doing to find her.

"I know you can hear me, Jane. Let me help," Steve pleaded.

The microphone would give her position away since they could hear everything around her. So she wrapped it in the note and shoved it in her pocket. Pulling the strands of the long red wig closer to her face, she joined a small group of bored teenagers headed in the direction of the Alamo's east exit.

Two men dressed in phone company shirts watched the gate. Probably FBI. She pushed her hands in her pockets and stuck close to the family ahead of her, turning toward the parking lot on the opposite corner.

She flattened against the parking garage wall and covertly returned the earpiece to her ear. When she heard that the agents didn't see her leave through the gate, she circled the block and entered the Menger.

"Palmer, running is not the answer. Give us the boy and we'll get you the help you need."

"McCaffrey, get off this frequency. This is my op."

"You've lost her, Woods, and your badge."

"I didn't hear a fat lady sing, McCaffrey."

Steve's anger made Jane flinch. He was in a lot of trouble, but once she got Rory, she'd turn herself in and make things right. She replaced the earpiece in her pocket.

One of the oldest hotels in the South, the Menger filled an entire city block. It was easy to gain access through one of the specialty shops that faced the street. An elderly man and woman sat with their drinks in the lobby and didn't glance twice at her when she walked to the desk.

"May I help you?" a young man in a hotel vest asked from behind the counter.

"Yes. I believe you have a message for Rhonda Fraser?"

The clerk pulled a letter-size envelope from beneath the counter and slid it to her without a word.

"Thank you."

Following the sign to the restroom, Jane locked the door to the single stall. She took the first calm breath since leaving the building across from the Alamo where the FBI set up that morning.

What was she doing? Trying to outsmart the FBI? Her? No, she was a mother determined to get her son back. And if that meant running from the U.S. Marine Corps, she would.

Rory was the single most important thing in her life. She couldn't let him down. Her hands were shaking when she withdrew the earpiece again to listen.

"The perp must have left her a disguise, sir."

"Woods isn't answering, sir. He left our line of sight at the east exit."

She couldn't recognize the voices. She ripped the end of the envelope and took another deep breath before unfolding the paper.

A ticket floated to the floor.

Ripley's Believe It or Not Wax Museum.
Mother Goose Exhibit.
NOW.

"Check every taxi, car, truck," McCaffrey commanded.

"We don't have the manpower—"

"They aren't far. Lanning, I want them back in custody within the hour. Find them."

Listening only long enough to verify they weren't outside the door, she hid the earpiece in her pocket again. The ball cap went into the trash can before she headed back to the clerk in the lobby.

"Can I help you, Miss Fraser?"

"It's getting so sticky outside." She pulled the wig's long hair off her neck. "Do you have a couple of rubber bands?"

"Sure. No problem."

"Thanks."

Pulling the wig into two sections, she braided the strands to hang on either side of her face. She headed across the street, downstairs from the very building she'd begun her journey from that morning. The wax museum was just below the offices utilized by the FBI. She waited until a man in a suit, obviously an agent, exited a tour bus before she entered. He didn't look back and walked onto a second sightseeing bus which hid the Alamo from her—and her from the agents still interviewing bystanders.

The noise in the lobby of the wax museum was phenomenal. Arcade games clanged and beeped. Indistinguishable music piped into the open lobby. People spoke louder to be heard. Jane placed her hand over her jeans pocket to muffle the noise. The line wasn't too long, only taking a couple of minutes to gain entrance to the exhibits.

The dark didn't give her comfort. In fact, the eerie way John Wayne's eyes followed her made the hair on the back of her neck stand up. Someone watched her in the winding hall. She hurried through, trying not to stare at the lifelike images.

A flash from a camera sparked the darkness, causing her eyes to have to adjust again.

The Three Stooges. Elvis. Redford and Newman in a scene from *The Sting*. Marlon Brando. But no Mother Goose. She walked as fast as the patrons allowed her. The line bottle-necked at a sales counter and the *Wizard of Oz* display.

It was so tempting to pull out the earpiece and whisper to the agents where she was. Fear for her son's safety kept her mouth shut and her feet moving through the next set of doors.

Then she was in the wonderland of Mother Goose. She stopped so fast a guy bumped her from behind.

"Excuse me," he said politely.

"I'm sorry, it was my fault." Was he the kidnapper? She scanned his homely face suspiciously. He stepped around her and looked at the opposite display.

Nursery rhymes came to life with the *Old Lady Who Lived in a Shoe* and *Jack Be Nimble* jumping over a candlestick.

A woman with a small child pointing at the *Dish Running Away with the Spoon* stood at the end of the room. Was she the kidnapper? Did she hold the Brant child in her arms? No. The man who had bumped into Jane draped his arm around the woman and gave the child a kiss.

"Daddy," the little girl said with glee.

Stop overreacting and think. There must be a message here somewhere.

Her eyes desperately searched for a note and caught sight of a mailbox in the exhibit. That had to be it. After the family in front of her moved into the next room, she leaned over the rail and retrieved a note addressed to Rhonda Fraser.

Mittman and Dilworth.
SW Corner House.

If her knees hadn't been locked, she would have landed face-first on the worn black carpet. How was she supposed to get there? The kidnapper had made certain she didn't have any cash, credit cards or identification when she left Dallas. And even if he hadn't, no one with the FBI would give her cab fare.

Beg, hitch a ride, hot-wire a car? All the book learning in the world still required money or a set of keys to get from one point to another. Or maybe she should wait for Steve at the Hilton. Involve him further? Trust him? Could he help her without letting the rest of the FBI know what was going on?

Get to some light, make sure the envelope is empty. Then she would make a decision. Following the path, she ventured through another set of doors and there he was.

Leaning against the frame of an emergency exit, his legs crossed at the ankles, one hand on his hip, Steve's smile waited along with the rest of him.

Something snapped inside her. She literally saw red for the first time in her life. How dared he stand there looking smug in his knowledge that she hadn't avoided him as she'd hoped?

Well, he wouldn't stop her from following the kidnapper's instructions to the letter this time. She ran full force at him, barreling into his body with every bit of her strength.

The scream seemed far in the distance, but she realized it was hers as it suddenly cut off when her breath was knocked from her chest. They fell through the door to the outside sunlight and the scream was replaced by an alarm.

"What have I done?" she asked herself as people began running toward them. "I need money for a cab."

"We've got to get out of here. Fast. Did you get another note?" Steve asked. "You're not going alone."

Steve took her hand and hauled her to her feet. The look on Jane's face when she'd laid eyes on him was unforgettable. Fury. Plain and simple. It was good to see a strong emotion from her. He just hadn't planned on it shoving him through the fire exit.

They ran through the alley away from the Alamo. Steve's

only hope was to get lost on the River Walk in the crowd. They could emerge several streets south by the convention center and catch a cab to wherever the kidnapper had instructed her to go.

Their getaway was cut short.

Stubblefield—and the Glock she pointed at Steve's chest—caused him to jerk to a stop, pulling Jane with him.

"What's wrong with you?" she asked, looking at him. Out of the corner of his eye, he saw her slowly turn and look.

"Put your hands where I can see them," Stubblefield said.

Stubblefield was alone, jacket off, gun in her hand. To get Jane away, he'd have to overpower his former partner and risk being shot. And he had no doubt that she'd shoot. But he couldn't just give up.

"We're not armed." He raised his hands into the air. Jane followed his lead. "Give me this one, Selena. It's Jane's son. I need to find him."

His former partner raised her brow, obviously wondering what he was up to since she'd verified Rory was dead. But she kept the gun at her side, no longer pointing it at anyone.

"We have an audience." She nodded behind them. Employees from the wax museum and onlookers had backed to the opposite end of the alley when Selena had showed her weapon.

"Then I'll just have to force you to let us go." He smiled as cheerfully as he could fake.

Jane looked from him to the gun to the people behind them and back to Stubblefield.

He shoved Jane to the side, then leaped toward his FBI team member.

She fired a shot wide and into the brick. Stubblefield didn't miss unless it was intentional.

He took as much of the force as he could from the tackle and fall to the pavement. "Why are you helping me?"

"I'm giving you a chance, Steve. Don't louse it up."

"Run, Jane. I'm right behind you," he shouted, and she took off without a word. With the crowd growing, he'd lose her in a matter of seconds.

"You need to make this look real. My cuffs are behind my back," Stubblefield said. "Don't take too long, cowboy. Call me on my cell."

"Will do. Thanks. I owe you." He snapped the cuffs around her wrist and hauled her to a nearby car, locking the other metal bracelet around the steering wheel. Then he took off like a bull out of the shoot.

He caught Jane at the next intersection.

"Ditch the wig and earpiece in a trash can."

Removing the red eyesore, she hit him in the chest with it. They crossed the street and took the steps down to the River Walk. It would be very easy to lose a tail along the winding maze of sidewalks lined with restaurants and shops for the tourists of San Antonio.

"Where are we headed?" he asked, dumping the wig in the garbage along with the earpieces. Replacing those would probably come out of his last FBI check.

"I have to go alone."

"I said…" He grabbed her arm, causing her to come to an abrupt stop. "Where are *we* going?"

"I need money for a cab, Steve. That's all. The note said to come alone."

"I know it's a risk, but there's no f—" He grimaced, took a deep breath, let go of her arm and she fell into step beside him. "There's no way I'm letting you go on your own. Get used to the idea. So if you want a cab, tell me where we're going."

"The southwest corner house at Dilworth and Mittman," she said.

"Did they give you a time limit?"

She shook her head.

"There are plenty of cabs at the convention center. I suppose they'll know how to get there."

"It's approximately three miles from here." Her eyes closed as she barely paused to retrieve the rest of the information from her extraordinary brain. "Mittman runs north and south, the intersection is approximately one-point-six miles from Interstate 37, which is approximately point-eight miles from the convention center." She spoke the information as if everyone in the city should know how many eighths of a mile they were from the interstate.

"When did you take a look at a city map?"

"This morning at the Bureau. There was one on the wall. Don't worry, I can extrapolate the information up here—" she tapped her head "—and actually use it."

He didn't doubt her. Any moment he expected a small army of .45s to be aimed at them. He kept one eye on the rock pathway that wound around the river and the other on the street level wall.

"You going to share those notes now?" He slowed down behind a line forming for lunch at one of the many restaurants on the river. He stuck out his hand expecting Jane to place the kidnappers' messages there.

"Are you going to tell me how you knew where I was?" She shoved her hand in her jeans pocket, stared at him a second, but turned and kept the notes.

"No-brainer." He shrugged, placed his empty hand behind her back and hurried her along. "I followed you."

The roasted peppery Tex-Mex smells from the restaurants tried to distract him. But he was concentrating on the notes, the kidnappers, Rory, bad guys, the Brant kid and Jane. How had the kidnappers known everything about their operation this morning? How could they have figured out where all their agents would be?

"So how did you get ahead of me? I would have noticed you passing by in the confining exhibits."

"I didn't. Pass by you, that is. I flashed my badge and went through the exit, then spied you at Mother Goose when the family ahead of you left the area. Now what do the notes say?"

Several minutes of silence went by as they walked along the river's cobblestone sidewalk. They passed small groups of people wearing convention badges. Small groups of people intent on their conversations. Steve couldn't see anyone watching them intently, or following—even at a distance.

"They gave directions on how to get by your friends. The last note said to get to Mittman and Dilworth." She said the words as if all kidnappers deliver ransom notes in a wax museum.

Leaving the gathering lunch crowd behind, he adjusted his long strides to fit Jane's pace. She was tired. The dark circles under her eyes weren't smeared mascara. She'd been through the wringer. At least they were walking in the cool shade by the river.

"They told you where to go, but left no cash for you to get there?"

"No."

Did the kidnappers want her to fail? Or walk. She said it was less than three miles. Maybe they needed time?

He quickened their pace and made it to the end of the river by the convention center. But before he took her the approximate two and a quarter miles to the danger zone he needed to know something. "Would you have met me at the Hilton?"

She looked at her feet. He knew the answer, but couldn't understand why she was reluctant to say it. She'd come to him before, had said that she trusted him again. So what was the problem?

"I put Rory in danger. Now you're in jeopardy of losing your career and we still may not find him."

What could he say? Everything would be all right when he found Rory. He pulled her close, searching her eyes for a sign. A glimmer that she knew her son was more important than his job.

As if magnets pulled them together, his lips found hers

and he kissed her for all he was worth. He could lose himself in the luscious, soft silkiness of her mouth. Why hadn't he done this the moment he'd seen her? Nothing had changed between them. She kissed him back as if the past four years hadn't happened.

Her warmth was different than the heat surrounding him. It didn't drain him like the sun's rays. It revitalized him, gave him energy to keep going.

Hot damn, she felt good.

This was where he belonged. Where Jane belonged. Things would be set to rights again. She had to forgive him eventually.

Didn't she?

"We…um…" Her hands frantically pushed at his chest. "We can't do this now. Where's a cab?"

Maybe the timing wasn't the best in the world. If it were his kid missing, the only thing he'd be thinking about was finding the bastard that took him. But having her in his arms again felt completely right.

Chapter Seven

"Are you out of your mind, woman?" Steve asked the air while taking both steps to the porch in one jump.

Stick to the plan. He'd preached it for the past ten minutes in the cab. Stick to *his* plan. The plan where he burst in the door. A door she shouldn't enter under any circumstances.

Sticking to Jane's plan would get them killed. She was in the dilapidated house alone, ignoring specific instructions he'd given her. They didn't know who or what was waiting where the kidnappers had arranged to meet her.

No one had answered her timid knock and she'd rushed inside…alone. Unarmed. *Her* plan was to have him stay out of sight on the opposite corner. He was out of position because of her enthusiasm and his cautiousness.

The screen slapped him in the butt as he stopped at a set of shoes—toes pointing toward the ceiling. An old lady was flat on her back, eyes staring blank at the ceiling.

"Jane?"

Hurried footsteps in one of the back rooms made him wish for his .45. He'd run the operation this morning so he could protect Jane, but McCaffrey had refused to release his weapon. He should have insisted. Then he wouldn't feel so powerless. Jane ran into the room and he could breathe again. He hoped to high heaven that no one else was in the house.

For a split second he believed the boy in her arms was Rory. The way she cradled the toddler's body close to hers was like an experienced mother. But it was the Brant child that turned to face him.

Thrusting the small sniffling child into his hands, Jane stepped over the dead woman and continued around the corner.

"Uh…Jane?" He followed her into the tiny kitchen where she frantically opened each cabinet door leaving them swinging on their hinges. Thomas Brant squirmed, clearly not liking the awkward tension of hands holding him.

He tried to soften his hold, but face it, he'd been undercover and missed being around his niece and nephew when they were this age.

"He's not here. There's no one here. There's no note telling me where to go." Jane sank to the floor and burst into tears. She wrapped her arms around herself and rocked, a forlorn keening sound rising from her throat that sent a chill down his spine.

The child in his arms seemed stunned and didn't move. Steve couldn't move either. Thoughts of Rory paralyzed him, robbing him of positive words she needed to hear. As quickly as she'd lost it, she stopped all the emotion and didn't react at all.

"What have they done with him?" She wiped her eyes with her palms and stood. She looked up at him, her eyes as dead as the woman's on the floor.

Yeah, it finally registered the woman wasn't moving. Right, he was the decorated FBI agent. The one who should have checked for a pulse when he came through the door.

The toddler began to whimper. The kid would be howling louder than a lonesome coyote in a matter of seconds. He handed him back to Jane and knelt by the big grandmotherly-type woman. No pulse. Yep, deader than a doornail, but not quite cold. No blood. No visible wound.

He worked the room. No signs of a struggle. The vic's clothes weren't disordered. No broken glass from windows. But the door had crept open when Jane knocked on it. No facial contortions, no apparent bruising around the neck indicating strangulation.

"This your neighbor?"

"She was so kind to us." Jane looked around the room. "I don't understand it. Some of Rory's things are here. A couple of toys, his cereal bowl." She pointed to the yellow plastic Cheerio on the high chair.

A very expensive-looking wooden high chair that didn't match the run-down appearance of the rest of the house.

"It's his. He colored on it with my green Sharpie." She patted the back of the child in her arms. "This little one is wearing Rory's shirt."

"Thomas Brant."

Jane shifted from foot to foot while patting the little guy's back. The kid quieted in an instant.

Steve took a closer look, taking in details, trying to guess why Jane was led here. There had to be a reason, a reason for everything. A reason the kidnappers wanted the FBI to believe Jane was crazy. But what? He paced the room and gave the woman another glance. What had killed her? She had no obvious marks or wounds. Maybe they injected her with some type of poison. Injected her? Just like Jane injected him. Coincidence?

"Damn!"

One bowl of Cheerios on the high chair, another plastic bowl in the sink. Three half-filled cups of juice on the counter. A blanket in the playpen along with two teddy bears. But the small trash can overflowed with used diapers. He wasn't an expert, but that looked like an excessive amount for one three-year-old.

"Son of a b— I played right into their hands." The house hadn't been tossed. The body was still warm. His instincts should have kicked him in the head to get him moving a little sooner. "Jane, we have to get out of here. Someone's framing you for murder."

"What? But we can't leave." She looked at the child in her arms.

"I'm pretty sure the police will be here any minute, ready to arrest you. Someone has gone to a lot of trouble to make it look like you were crazy." He turned her toward him and searched her eyes. Her wonderful innocent eyes. "Trust me on this, Janie. We've got to go."

"But what about Thomas? We can't just leave—"

"He'll be fine in the playpen. We can't take him with us. It really would be kidnapping."

Sirens sounded in the distance. The police weren't keeping their arrival a secret.

"Now, Jane." He took the toddler and ran him to the playpen in the corner. "Go! Out the back door. Fast!"

"I don't understand. Why isn't there a note telling us where Rory is? How are we going to find him? What do they want now?"

You behind bars, paying for their crimes.

"I promise I'll answer all of your questions as soon as we're clear of the cops. Now go." He punched George's speed dial and tossed the department-issued cell on the floor to guide his team to the house.

Risking precious time, he looked closely at Mrs. Newinsky's arms and found what appeared to be a puncture wound. He was almost certain that she'd been killed with the same formula that had paralyzed him less than two days ago. The kidnappers had stolen Jane's serum along with the Brant ransom and were using it against her.

No time to search the house for the money, but it wouldn't be here.

Someone had gone to a lot of trouble to frame Jane. They just weren't counting on him being around to help her.

CLIMBING THEIR SEVENTH FENCE, Jane accepted Steve's lift to get her over the top and promptly plopped onto the thick carpet of St. Augustine grass. He, on the other hand, hit the ground running, coming back when he realized she hadn't followed.

"I'm sorry, Steve. I just can't do this anymore. My legs are like jelly."

"This is the only way."

"Can we hide? Sit for a moment?"

Steve hadn't said anything since leaving that house. He must hate her. Could she forgive him if he'd cost her career? And when she told him Rory was his son…what then? Even if he didn't, she hated herself enough for the both of them and no longer cared if she got caught.

Without another note she didn't have any clue how to find Rory. And as long as he was running, Steve couldn't find him, either.

"Let me stay in this yard until they find me. It'll give you time to get away." She nodded to a shed in the corner. "You know, one or two fences from now, a Doberman is going to be waiting." Smiling kept her from crying another flood. She had to have *some* self-respect around this man.

"Jane—"

"Please don't. I know you hate me."

"I don't hate you. Why would I hate you?" He pulled on her arm, trying to get her to stand. "Shoot, there's another patrol car. Come on."

"We can't outrun them."

"We aren't going to. See if the shed's unlocked and if there's a lawn mower inside."

"What are—"

"We're going to hide in plain sight."

"What if they're home, for goodness' sake?" she asked, but kept running toward the shed.

"Then we're sunk, babe." But he looked in the kitchen window and carefully walked through the gate and looked in front.

Jane pulled the lawn mower and gas can out the door.

There were gardening gloves, a floppy hat and a baseball cap on a shelf so she grabbed those, too. Seeing the shears, she poked a hole in her jeans leg and cut. She pulled and ripped the remaining pants leg, then threw them in the far corner of the building.

Steve had his shirt off and pulled the water hose from where it hung neatly at the side of the house. He stuck his head under the water and plastered his hair back. Then reached for the cap and tucked his longish strands under it.

"Take your bra off and knot your shirt between your breasts."

"What?" She couldn't believe what he asked.

"Just do it, Jane. I hope if a cop does stop that it's a guy."

Like most girls, she learned at an early age how to take off her bra without removing her shirt. Even though it was a sports bra, she managed to pull her arms through, stuff it in her back pocket and knot the T-shirt, exposing her belly.

A scream escaped when Steve turned the cold stream on her. "What are…" Her mouth filled with water.

"You're the distraction, babe." He had the gall to smirk before he shut the faucet off.

"If I ever have the opportunity to finish this water fight, beware." She couldn't think of anything appropriate while she wiped the moisture from her eyes.

She heard the mower start behind her and hoped no one thought it odd that a Texan would be mowing his yard on a hot July day, in long pants and a worn pair of cowboy boots.

With the floppy hat pushed as low on her head as it would go, the gardening gloves and the pruning shears, she marched to the rose bushes bordering the front hurricane fence and trimmed. Determined to look as if she knew what she was doing, she snipped withering buds as fast as she could and let them fall to the ground.

A patrol car passed.

Then it backed up.

Oh, God.

What would she do? She couldn't lie her way out of a paper bag.

The officer got out of his car and walked toward her. So absorbed in the policeman, she didn't register that Steve had cut the engine until his warm arms spun her around to face him. The direction of his eyes fell to her lips. He was going to kiss her.

Not just a passing peck on the cheek or a casual "take care" kiss. But a real one. She recognized the look from their brief affair. That was how he'd looked *every* time he'd kissed her back then.

Had time stopped? If it hadn't, why was it taking him so long to bend his head and connect with her? She rose on her tiptoes and felt the soul-jerking wrench of her body aching for more as soon as their lips met. She parted her mouth and tried to bring him closer.

It wasn't just her. Steve wanted her, too. He couldn't hide his reaction or the sound of pleasure vibrating from his body to hers. His hands were just bringing their bare skin even closer when the patrolman cleared his throat.

Steve raised an eyebrow and took a step back. "Hey, sorry, honey. I didn't realize we had company. Can we help you, Officer?"

He casually hooked the T-shirt around his neck and pulled on both ends. She wanted to concentrate on the way his muscles grew when he reached over his head or just how good he looked. After all, four years was a long time. And good grief, that kiss. Was she really supposed to think now?

"You two been outside long?"

Steve put an arm around her bare waist. "What, about an hour?"

Jane nodded and kept the brim of the hat between her face and the officer's gaze. A gaze that rarely left her breasts. There wasn't much there, but everything she had was outlined by the wet T-shirt. Including her now-erect nipples. Willpower kept her arms at her sides instead of across her chest. Fortunately they'd given her a dark blue T-shirt that morning.

"Winnie, do we have any iced tea in the fridge?" Steve pinched her behind to get a response to the strange name.

It could have been worse. He could have called her Winifred.

"I think so…Fred. Do you need a drink?"

"Yeah. Could we offer you a glass?" he asked the officer.

"No, thank you, sir. We're looking for a man and woman. They're armed and considered dangerous. I need to get back to the search."

"Dang." Steve drew out the four letters like only a Southern man could. "Really? What did they do? Is Winnie in danger?" He draped his arm across her shoulders and pulled her close to his side. "I told you we shouldn't have moved to this neighborhood."

The teasing look in his eyes encouraged her to play along. "You were the one who wanted to move closer to your mother, dear."

"Should we go inside and call 911 if we see any strangers?" Steve asked the policeman. "You said they have guns?"

"Yes. I need to be on my way." With one last look at her chest, the officer left.

As soon as the car was out of sight, Jane elbowed Steve in his stomach.

"Ooomph."

"And just how was I supposed to get into a locked house and get that tea?"

"I was betting that he wouldn't accept, darlin'."

"And what if you were wrong, *Fred?*"

"I would have kidded you a lot about locking us out of the house, *Winnie*." The smile he flashed made what was left of her heart melt. It seemed so genuine, as if he were actually flirting with her. He pulled the back door to the garage open. "Now for some transportation."

"You aren't seriously considering stealing?"

"I'm not going to steal a thing," he said as he took a screwdriver to the inside door. "We're just going to use the phone."

"That's all?"

"Gee, *Winnie,* I thought *I* was the federal agent."

Jane couldn't bring herself to enter the house. She stood dripping at the garage door and watched for the police, a neighbor or the owners of the cute little home with the yellow rosebushes she'd butchered.

"All done, cab will be here in half an hour." Steve lifted an arm as if he were about to drop it across her shoulders, but he changed his mind and direction. "You didn't touch anything, did you?" he asked as he stepped down into the yard again.

"Just the shears. And the rest of my jeans are in the shed."

"That was quick thinking." He eyed her legs, then her wet T-shirt. His hungry look made her unknot the wet material and tuck it into her new shorts. He laughed at her grimace when the cold touched her heated skin. "Let me put away the lawn mower, wipe everything down, then we're going to talk."

She handed him the borrowed gardening supplies. Her eyes were glued to his sculpted back and swaggering hips until he disappeared into the shed.

Quit it.

Concentrate. Remember how the house looked. Remember everything inside. Imprint your horrible brain with the picture.

But that wasn't a problem. She could answer anything about the way that house looked. Anything. Especially how Mrs. Newinsky's eyes had been staring at her as beady as a dead lab rat.

Half an hour to talk. Where would they begin? More important, where would they go from here? She sat in a covered swing near the corner of the yard by the rosebushes.

"What did you mean back at the house when you said someone was framing me for murder?" she asked him across the yard. "What went wrong? Why leave the Brant baby and not Rory? It doesn't make sense. Do they expect me to pay a ransom, too? I have a little money from my parents' estate, but not anything close to the million the kidnappers have already received."

"Quiet." He popped out from behind the door, shut it and sauntered toward her. "Want everyone and their mothers to hear you?"

"What did you mean?"

Sitting next to her, he hesitated—as if he didn't want to frighten her. He'd acted that way when he told her to take the job at Johns Hopkins.

"I think the kidnappers' accomplice, the woman you knew as Mrs. Newinsky, was killed with your serum. Whoever did this went to a heckuva lot of trouble."

"I don't understand."

"There's something I couldn't tell you yesterday." He leaned forward on his knees, stopping the natural motion of the swing. "I tried to get you alone, but McCaffrey wouldn't let me see you again. By then…"

"What is it?"

Steve watched her dark blue eyes dart back and forth, barely blinking in their intensity. All he wanted was to kiss her. The blood surged away from his brain, but he knew he couldn't act like a seventeen-year-old kid.

How could he say this without her falling apart again? The kidnappers didn't intend to return Rory and she needed to know.

Damn it, she probably already knew. He didn't know how to say it delicately even though he'd said something similar exactly nine times before.

"Whoever arranged Rory's kidnapping forged a death certificate. For Rory. That he died three months ago. They made it look like you kidnapped Thomas Brant as a substitute for your son."

She didn't say a word.

"We received a doctor's record of you being on antipsychotics. No record of a Mrs. Newinsky in your building. Add that not one thing was left in your apartment to indicate a child was ever there and it looked like Rory never existed."

"I see." Her mouth formed a tiny *O* as she shook her head. "You think I'm crazy."

"No. No, I never doubted you," he said firmly.

"But the FBI does." She stood out of his reach and covered her face with her hands, then miserably dropped them again.

"They're following the evidence, Jane." *I followed my heart and every instinct in my body that told me you wouldn't lie* He wanted to say it out loud. But couldn't. Not yet. Not until they found her son. He stayed on the swing, pushing away the need to hold her.

"They're not searching for him. No one's searching for him. Last night...with the camera. You...that's why you told me to run to the Hilton. Oh, my God. They all think I'm crazy."

"I keep saying this, but we *will* find him. I swear if it's the last thing I ever do, I'll find Rory."

He *would* find Rory and return him to his mother. A mother that he'd prove had nothing to do with the Brant kidnapping. He'd prove it whether employed by the Bureau or not. Confident? Cocky? He'd been called that before. This was more important than anything he'd ever done and he wouldn't let Jane or her son down.

"How?"

"We'll find him." He thought better on his feet and began to pace. "Our highest priority at the moment is getting out of here without leaving a trail. I have fourteen hundred dollars in cash but that won't last long. We can't risk a bank now."

"Do you always travel with that much cash?" She was carrying on a coherent conversation with him, but he could tell her mind was sorting through facts.

"I withdrew it last night."

"So you thought something would go wrong?"

He couldn't answer that. But withdrawing everything in his checking account had been a precaution he wished he hadn't been right about.

"I have a friend who owes me a favor. He should be somewhere in San Antonio. He'll be able to loan me money and a car."

"You've done this before?"

He stopped. "No, but I've chased a lot of men who have."

"Did any of them evade you and your team?"

"No, Jane. They didn't." He clenched his teeth. Sometimes her being so smart was a major pain in the ass.

"And why would we be any different?"

"Because I know how my team works. I know their standard procedures. Shoot, I wrote the procedures."

"I have a suggestion."

"Yeah?"

"Since the FBI assumed Rory was…um…you know."

He could see how difficult it was for her to even think the thought. He'd experienced it himself yesterday. She needed to be held, comforted and reassured everything would be okay. But he kept his distance. He needed to think.

Swallowing hard, she continued, "Most likely they didn't confer with anyone near my apartment. Any person there could have confirmed that Rory existed."

"The team didn't have a reason for interviews when they saw the death certificate."

"Why didn't they ask me?"

"The shrink advised against it."

"Yeah. So much for evidence." She pulled her arms tighter around her body, retreating further into a protective shell. "I have a…a friend. He'll wire me as much cash as we need."

A friend?

"Hayden won't ask questions, if that's what you're worried about."

"Huh?"

"There's no reason for that look on your face. I can trust Hayden."

The cab honked its arrival.

"Listen, we're Winnie and Fred. Got it?" Her head bobbed up and down. He was surprised the tears filling her eyes didn't bounce out. "And you do what I say."

"I'm not blindly following you anywhere, Agent Woods."

Just where she dredged up that spunk, he didn't care. They needed it. She needed it to get through the next few days.

"There's no debate here, sweetheart. When I say jump, you ask how high while you're already in the air." He pressed his lips into a thin line and nodded his head, agreeing with himself. "Yeah, you just remember who's in charge."

"Sure, Fred."

Chapter Eight

Jane had never been more scared in her life. Not for herself. But for Rory.

Every heartbeat seemed to take her farther from her son.

Every minute lessened the chance she'd ever find him.

The cheap motel walls shook each time a plane took off at Kelly Air Force Base. Even the sound of jet engines wouldn't interfere with some sleep if Steve would just stop pacing. Back and forth. Side to side. The same short length of carpet would be even more threadbare than when they arrived.

"I don't understand," she said as she fell to the bed, so tired she could barely move. "Why such an elaborate scheme to make me look crazy? Who would want the FBI to think Rory was dead?"

"Don't you get it? Someone not only wants your son, but they want to put you away for life. And, honey, in Texas, murder might make your life real short. Understand?"

"The death penalty." Yes, she understood.

"So let's go over it again," he demanded. "Do you have anyone who wants you and Rory out of the picture? Who benefits from your serum if it's not you?"

"I don't know, Steve. I've told you this." She hit the bed with her palms and sat up. "I haven't made a will and the formula isn't in the moneymaking stage yet, but I suppose it would all go to Rory."

Between each question, she grew more and more certain

there wouldn't be a request for ransom. More concerned each minute she stayed awake. She needed sleep. But there was no way to rest. Not until her son was back in her arms.

With her eyes, she wearily followed Steve's habitual pacing. Up and down from the door to the bathroom—between the full-size bed and the cheap mirror on the dresser. His reflection doubled the annoying habit.

"Don't you ever get tired?" she asked. "If you can let my brain recharge, I'll be able to keep up."

"We're missing something," he said. "Let's go over it again."

At least his voice sounded tired but his actions were jerky. He held the bridge of his nose, squeezing his eyes shut for a moment. He was running on sugar and caffeine. They both were. She craved the weight of the covers on top of her, but she wouldn't sleep. Logic told her she should get as much sleep as possible. She needed to rest in order to search for Rory.

If the police burst in the door at this point, she'd promise to be here in the morning if they just let her sleep for several hours straight.

"I've been awake since Wednesday at 5:00 a.m. It's now sometime around two on Friday afternoon. I could determine how many hours I've been awake, but honestly, I don't want to know." She toed off each shoe, pulled back the covers and plumped the unfamiliar pillows. "Zombies have more energy than I do."

Curling her legs between the cool sheets, stretching her back flat and laying her head on a pillow were ordinary little things. She just needed to rest her eyes. Then begin again.

"As much as I want Rory back in my arms, you've convinced me there's nothing to do until we meet your friend. When you called, he said to meet him at the mall at nine. So we rest."

To give him credit, he didn't talk anymore. His pacing, however, didn't slow. Attempting to block him from sight, she covered her head and heard the bathroom door open then quietly shut. The pipes rattled, signaling the use of the shower.

I sure hope he knows what to do next. They were putting their freedom at risk by avoiding the authorities.

The drums pounding in her head wouldn't stop, and she just couldn't speculate anymore. The headache was partly from exhaustion, partly from thinking so hard, and partly from questioning everything that had happened. She'd been set up, but by whom?

She didn't have enemies. Nor friends—other than Hayden. And he didn't need her formula. Hayden Hughes came from a long line of old money and didn't need to work at all.

Friends had been a void in her life from the time she could recite everything read or taught to her. No playgroups for Mom and Dad's special girl. No lasting friendships, no family, no terrific teachers, no nothing except one move after another.

Well, Rory would have more. She'd brought him back to Dallas to meet his family. All of it, whether Steve liked it or not. Rory had a birthright and needed grandparents. She wouldn't demand Steve change his life, she couldn't ask that.

And as for Rory, nothing made sense. Who would want to take him from her?

Calm down. Sleep. Things had to be better when she could think clearly and use her brain to get out of this mess. Like her mother had constantly warned, her emotions interfered with logic and had to be kept at bay.

The room phone lay on the table next to the bed. Steve had specifically said not to contact anyone, but what happened if he changed his mind or if his team believed the death certificate was real? Who could help her?

Hayden.

Her fingers quickly tapped the keypad by memory. "Collect from Jane. Come on, Hayden. Pick up."

"Yes, I'll accept. Hello?"

The familiar voice brought a warmth to her inside she hadn't felt since returning from the store to find men in her apartment.

"I don't have time to completely explain, Hayden. I need you to contact the FBI and verify that you know Rory was alive when I last saw you."

"Jane? What's happened? I don't understand."

"Rory's been kidnapped." The sound of a friendly, caring voice was enough for the tears to build in her eyes again.

"Oh, my God, who would do something like that? What do they want? Do you need money? I can leave Baltimore and be there in a matter of hours."

"I don't know why this is happening, Hayden."

"Why do you need me to verify Rory's alive, Jane? Where are you?"

"It's too complicated. Rory was taken to San Antonio. We're meeting someone who can help us later tonight at a mall."

"Who's we? Are you with Rory's father?"

"Yes. Steve's helping me. I can't explain." She could understand his frustration. She heard the water shut off. "Please, I'm begging you, contact the FBI and tell them about Rory. I have to go."

She placed the phone gently on the receiver and pulled the covers over her shoulder.

The door opened and closed again.

"I'm too tall to sleep in the bathtub."

If she ignored him, maybe—just maybe—he'd assume she *was* asleep.

"You gave yourself away by holding your breath before you decided to pretend you were out. This isn't up for discussion. It's a warning. I'm coming out of this bathroom in my shorts and climbing into that bed."

Exhausted, she was determined to force herself to sleep. She'd never find Rory if her mind couldn't focus. She kept her eyes closed tight. At least that was what she kept telling herself to do even when she peeked at Steve's long legs and bare chest.

AFTER HE'D CRAWLED INTO BED, he'd finally managed a deep sleep. Between listening to every car door in the parking lot and consciously knowing Jane's luscious body lay next to him, it was difficult to close his eyes.

It was evening. Proof of it shone through the window where the privacy curtains overlapped. A streetlight beam fell directly across Steve's face, causing him to squint his eyes shut.

A steady stream of fighter planes shook the building until he wanted to protect his head when the roof caved in. But it held together and normal traffic sounds came through the walls.

Attempting to stretch into action, he realized he was lightly pinned on his right side. Sometime during their rest, he'd wrapped Jane in his arms. Or she'd laid her head on his chest. Either way it didn't matter. She was tensing by the millisecond so she must be awake.

She scampered away from him toward the edge of the bed, pulling most of the sheet with her.

"It's okay, sweetheart. You still have all your clothes on." He gave the top blanket a gentle tug in the direction of his lap. "I, on the other hand, do not."

He didn't want her to notice what she did to him. But he didn't have long to worry. Without a word, she slid off the bed and retreated to the bathroom.

"Nice waking up next to you, too, beautiful," he said when he heard the door shut behind her.

God, he missed her. Digging into work had filled the empty time he'd never noticed until after Jane was gone. It was stupid to think he was whole again. In all this mess, he didn't have the right to think of her in a physical way, but he just couldn't get her out of his head.

It took some doing, but he pulled on his jeans. He walked to the Texaco station across the street and bought two cups of coffee. At the last minute he remembered the two creams and sugars for Jane, hoping she still took it that way.

Standing in the laundry at the corner of the building, he waited several minutes before making his way back to the room. He was fairly certain no one had caught up with them yet—friend or foe. But it was only a matter of time. He'd trained George and eventually his team would check on Jane's story.

Eventually. But no one had checked yesterday and some-one's pay increase would be forfeit for that major mistake.

Jane sat on the edge of the bed in front of the TV finger-combing her hair when he entered their room again. The action stirred something deep within him. A memory of the first time they'd made love. Jane had showered and combed her hair the same way.

Until he'd tossed his brush in her lap.

That had been the beginning. Were they coming full circle to start again? Or were they on the verge of the end?

"Thanks," she said as he handed her the foam cup.

"I thought we'd hit the mall food court before we meet Rhodes."

"What's wrong with meeting him here? Besides the fre-quent fly-bys and thin-as-toilet-paper walls?"

"Rhodes has a place and should have a computer. We can't stay here long. It's only a matter of time until they track us."

"Right, I know how thorough your team is." She took a long slurp of coffee.

"Come on, Jane. Give me a break here."

She pointed the remote toward the TV and turned up the volume. "You're as big a celebrity as I am now."

His picture—a very drab FBI head shot taken years ago when his hair was academy-length short and he looked like a bald rooster—appeared in the corner of the screen as the news anchor said, "…was on medical leave. They're unsure if Palmer and her accomplice have abducted Agent Woods or if he is with them voluntarily."

A string of words his mother would have fainted upon hearing from his mouth blurred together and only "stupid McCaffrey" escaped.

"Why is he stupid? Now he has the entire state looking for us."

"Yeah! Right!" He couldn't seem to make his mouth work. His parents were going to freak. Kidnapped? On the run? He'd have to get a message to them soon. "Did McCaffrey try to call me and see what was going on?"

"Like you would have answered your phone between jumping over fences and mowing the lawn in your boots?" She giggled. "Besides, I saw you leave it so your team would find the Brant child sooner."

"We'll have to pick up a prepay phone at the mall." It was good to see her smile. "So, he still didn't try."

"What are your plans?" She pointed the remote and clicked off the news. "Where do we start? Do we dye our hair and get you a fake beard?"

"Sleep does you wonders."

So she wanted to get down to business. She was right. Had he really expected concern or sympathy? Yeah, he had. He wasn't thinking with the brain he'd trained to react quickly to the facts presented to him. Nope, he was allowing other parts of his anatomy to lead him around.

Gulping the last bit of his coffee, he stood straight and chucked the cup into the trash can two feet away from Jane's sexy legs. Down to business. Yeah, right.

Easier said than done.

The ache to capture Jane's mouth under his caused him to swallow hard. Several times. But he managed to get the feeling compartmentalized. Right now he focused on finding the perps who'd framed Jane and kidnapped her son.

"You aren't going to like this." He sat on the corner of the dresser. "I need to call Agent Stubblefield."

"No."

"Yes. She helped us get away this morning. We can give her Hughes's number and she can confirm that Rory is alive. I need to find out if they've traced the money. We don't have a choice. We need their technology."

"I don't trust them."

"It's the fastest way to find Rory. The FBI has countless resources—"

"That didn't do them a bit of good yesterday."

"Arguing won't get us anywhere."

"How could you have thought I was crazy?" Her voice was filled with hurt and anguish.

"Whoa. The team did, but for the record, I never believed what the shrink said."

"Why not?"

He could tell her everything that had gone through his mind.

"They presented a rock-solid case for the team. The shrinks said you were delusional. That your need to have Rory alive had grown so great that you kidnapped a boy and came to me for help."

"And you didn't believe them?" she asked.

"No, I didn't. You didn't need me when you found out you were pregnant. And only came to me in a roundabout way when Rory was kidnapped."

Where had *that* come from? She turned her back to him, but he could tell she swiped at her eyes. He felt two feet tall.

As quickly as the tears came, they were gone.

When had she become this emotionless, detached robot? The woman he knew had been happy, full of life and energy. Had the past couple of years made her shut down? Or was it just being around him? Maybe she was angry enough not to allow *her* emotions to get in the way.

Maybe he should force himself to do the same? But every

time he looked at her, something reminded him of what they'd had and made him crave it again.

She flipped her hair and fluffed. The subject was officially changed. He loved the soft ringlets and curls left when she let it dry naturally. If things were different, Jane would be worried it made her look too young.

He wished things *were* different. Then maybe they could try to patch things up. Or start over. But that might be hard considering she was a mother.

"I asked Hayden to call the FBI."

"You did what?" He saw red. Or green. He was unable to differentiate whether his anger stemmed from her initiative or the fact that she'd asked *Hayden* for help. "Is Hughes the father?"

"No," she said quickly but took a long pause before continuing. "He's only a friend who can verify Rory was alive two weeks ago. We need to know who forged Rory's death certificate. Right? So when do we meet your friend Rhodes? I could use that computer."

"Soon, but what makes you think—"

"I can break into Maryland county records. It won't be that big a deal."

"That big a deal? Oh, sure, we're wanted for kidnapping and God only knows what else. What's a little hacking into government files?"

Rest really had done her good. She didn't flinch at his tantrum, didn't even blink an eye. She'd already set a plan in motion and they were about to see it through. She pulled her shoes on, the ones he'd found after looking in two Walmart stores for her size.

"Do you have sources that might help trace the money? Other than your team at the FBI. Know any hackers?"

"Sure, but—"

She was smiling. At least with her mouth, it didn't quite reach her eyes. She had her own agenda and apparently felt more confident.

"If I call Hayden again, he can have a computer genius we know work on it from his end."

"We can't involve more people."

"*We* should be able to find Rory, Steve. We don't need your friends at the FBI."

Ouch. That stung. Even if she were right, he had to call his team. He had to let someone in authority know all the craziness that was happening.

"You use your hacker. I'll give Stubblefield a call." Her jerk to attention told him she didn't like his compromise. "We have to prevent an out-and-out manhunt, Jane. Deal?"

"Maybe. Realistically, how long can we avoid the FBI or some other San Antonio cop?"

"We can do what we need probably by late tomorrow. Prove that Rory exists, get proof we can deliver to the Bureau, and force them to continue the search. We might even get lucky and discover who wants you out of the picture."

"What happens after that?"

He shrugged as an answer, but knew that he'd turn himself in and play on the media for sympathy. He had to. He'd prove Rory was alive by bringing this Hayden fellow to Texas, especially if he had pictures of Rory. But he'd hide Jane first. Someplace no one would think of.

Jane knew what that shrug suggested. She'd never surrender herself while Rory was still missing. No matter what Steve did, she couldn't give up hope. She didn't care who she had to ask or what she had to do.

"Let's get going then. Where do we meet your friend?" she asked.

"Food court."

When had he become so jaded? The Steve she'd known was funny and optimistic, never letting anything get him down. Until she'd gotten that letter from Johns Hopkins. Even then, he wouldn't stand in the way of her potential career. A career that had been empty without his smile.

Determined not to go down self-pity lane, she tried to

squeeze past him to get to the door. But in the little space between the bed and the dresser his hands stopped her with a touch to her shoulders.

Conflicting emotions surged through her body. Steve's touch, whether strong or gentle, always evoked a deep response. She wanted him to get angry, so it would be easier to be in the same room with him. But his face was filled with concern and confusion.

"Don't do that, Steve."

His deep brown eyes bored their way through the barrier she tried to keep erected between them. A barrier that crumbled with every look in his direction.

"Don't do what?" he asked a bit too huskily, a bit too close to her personal space. A bit like he knew exactly what he was doing.

"That."

"Be specific." He pulled her a fraction of an inch closer to his body. "Tell me what's wrong."

"I...ah...nothing. We need to leave, that's all." She tried to step out of his way, but he mirrored her actions. The corners of his mouth tilted upward.

"Liar."

The word was a soft whisper across the side of her neck, and caused gooseflesh to rise on her arms. Gathering the energy to look into his concerned eyes, she fell forward a step when he suddenly released her.

It was better this way.

Better to keep her distance. Better to keep secret what his deep searching eyes did to her heart, what his touch did to her soul. Better not to allow herself to love him again.

Chapter Nine

"So was that a good deal for a BlackBerry knockoff?" Jane asked, trying to ease the device from Steve's hands without success.

"This is the first time I've loved prepaid phone plans. No credit check. No real name." Steve sat at an empty table in the middle of the mall food court, seemingly unconcerned that their pictures were a part of every news station's rolling headline.

"Don't you think we should go somewhere else?" She saw another security guard and ducked her head. "Somewhere less conspicuous?"

"Don't worry about it, Jane." He smiled, looking totally relaxed. "Your driver's license pic doesn't look a thing like you now. It actually looks like a college ID."

"Just because your hair is six inches longer than in your picture doesn't mean someone won't recognize you." Even with the sleep she'd grabbed that afternoon, the tension was making her edgy.

"That's why I got the hat." He adjusted the black Stetson low on his brow. "I'll get us some food."

Steve's boots clicked across the floor behind her as she scooped the phone into her hands and sat at the metal table. The sound of someone running made her swivel her seat to look.

"We're leaving." Steve grabbed the phone, turned it off before placing it in his shirt pocket, and helped her stand.

"You said not to worry—" She pulled at the straps on the over-the-shoulder bags they'd picked up for a couple of dollars but was thrown off guard when Steve pulled her into a store and covered her mouth.

His hand was warm, but the cold chill in his eyes told her all she needed to know. The FBI or police were looking for them inside the mall.

"Jane," he whispered, "that's George and he's headed this way."

"What do we do now?"

"Run." He took the bags from her shoulder. He interlocked their fingers on one hand and leveled his face with hers. "Don't let go, Jane. Not unless I tell you to leave me."

Hands together, they took off at a fast walk back into the flow of mall customers. Keeping pace with Steve's stride was quite a workout for her shorter legs. She tried not to be obvious when she sneaked a peak behind them. The suits were still there, but seemed to be headed down another hallway.

Steve pulled her behind him and looked over his shoulder every sixth or seventh step until they reached a candy shop with two front exits. He ducked behind a lollipop display and looked at her through the heart-shaped suckers.

"I don't think he saw us." He pulled his hat off and handed it to her to hold, then began rolling up the sleeves on his Western snap shirt. "Don't drop that."

Her parents had told her that a calm head would prevail in any situation. And she had to agree. In an emergency, it was the composed person who became the leader or hero. But right now, right this minute, all Jane wanted to do was burst out with hysterical laughter.

Their son had been kidnapped, the FBI was chasing them, someone wanted to frame her for murder and Steve had just asked her not to drop his hat. How absurd was that?

"Hey, that's a great hat." He must have caught sight of her

near hysteria because he beamed. That was the only word for it. She knew thousands of words and *beamed* was the only one that completely described the look on Steve's face.

Every part of his slender face lit up. She imagined that "frightened to death" had been the look to describe her, until he'd handed her his hat.

Looking around the corner of the shop, then back at her, he beckoned her closer.

"Yes?"

"That sign over there says we're headed toward the southeast exit. Can you search that wonderful brain of yours and find out where we'll be if we walk fast for about ten minutes?"

She took a deep calming breath and pulled up the map of San Antonio in her mind. "Due east, about two blocks?"

"Zig to the right a block."

"Nock and Sharmain."

"Great. I'll call and tell Rhodes to meet us there. Stay here while I check on where George is."

The pressure from his hand subsided, but she didn't release him. "No, we go together."

His head nodded once, then the warmth of his hand reassured her again.

"Okay, let's head toward the restrooms and the emergency exit through the hall." He pointed, looked, then cautiously entered the crowd. She followed, holding tight to his hand.

And his hat.

Had he really said "wonderful brain"? No one, other than her parents and Hayden, had ever called her freakish memory wonderful. Those who had known weren't friends. She had been a study to marvel at how much her brain could absorb. It would be different for Rory.

She watched the hall entrance twenty feet away while Steve checked the door. She expected the men in suits to follow and yell, "Freeze!" But two women entered the hall after them and she relaxed just a bit. Even if they did eye Steve's backside several times before they pushed the ladies' room door open.

"We'll have to go back," Steve said, turning her by the shoulders. "The door sounds an alarm. I didn't think we'd get this lucky. Mind getting another shirt out for me?" He dialed the cell. "I'm not sure if George saw me or not, but changing our appearance can't hurt."

She searched through a sack for a shirt they'd picked up at the Goodwill store.

"Here you go—" She froze. At the entrance of the hallway stood two Hispanic men pointing guns straight at her.

"Put your hands in the air," the taller man on the left said with a heavy Spanish accent. They weren't in suits and ties like most FBI agents.

Jane watched in horror as the shorter one tipped his gun toward her.

"Please do not obey," the taller guy begged with an evil grin. His presence shouted that he wanted to hurt her. "We were told we could play with you a bit."

Oh, my God! She stumbled back. "Who sent you?" Steve quickly stepped between her and the men. His arms were in the air and she put her hands at his waist to push him out of the way. She didn't want him to die for her.

She didn't want either of them to die.

Steve had a knife. He'd bought that silly Western vest so he could hide it in the waistband of his jeans. He firmly held his ground, but turned just close enough to her that she felt the handle.

If she were reading him correctly, he wanted her to pull the knife from its sheath. Her knuckles brushed the small of his back but her fingers hesitated.

"We are happy to let you watch us with her, *amigo*. First we must leave. *Vamanos*," one of the men said.

"Do it."

Steve's words must have been a command for her because he wasn't moving like the men ordered. She was glad she couldn't see the guns any longer or she might have chickened out. She concentrated on small, quick movements that would be hidden behind Steve and managed to remove the knife.

"I'm getting kind of tired here, fellas." He began lowering his arms.

"Quiero lastimarte!" the talkative one said. "Move forward. Slowly."

"Okay, okay. Just don't let your fingers get itchy. We're comin'." He took a few steps in slow motion, but then suddenly Steve had the knife in hand and moved like lightning. He kicked one man in the stomach and swept the other's feet into the air without losing the blade. "Run."

She clutched the bags to her chest and didn't wait. Neither did Steve. They ran through the shoppers to the nearest exit, passed through the doors with women screaming at the sight of Steve's knife. It registered that he told those screamers to get down and out of the way. But she kept running into the dark parking lot, between cars, toward the main road.

A bullet shattered glass somewhere behind them and she dove for cover behind a Ford Explorer. The men had obviously recovered, followed and wanted to finish them. Steve stopped beside her, looked around for several seconds, then pulled the cell from his pocket, thumbing a text message.

Breathing hard and clutching the stitch in her side, she asked, "Now what do we do?"

"As much as I hate it, we wait on the cavalry." He looked toward the mall entrance. "Or wait on George. He should have word about gunfire."

"But Agent Lanning will—" More glass shattered above their heads.

"Yeah, arrest us."

"Isn't there anything else we can do?"

A rumbling and revving of an engine pulled up next to them. "Hey, man, are those dudes shooting real bullets?" A twentysomething man with two-toned spiked hair craned his head from a truck window.

"It's about time, Rhodes!" Steve shouted over the truck's booming woofers.

"Need a lift?" Rhodes nodded his head like a bobble doll in time with the music, tapping his fingers on the steering wheel.

The old red truck was more Bondo than paint. It looked older than dirt and Jane's first thought was that they could probably run faster than the truck could roll. A bumper sticker reading You Can't Kill a Man Born to Hang was slapped haphazardly over a dent in the door. More sayings were stuck to the bottom of the rear window.

Bullets peppered the asphalt between her and the truck, drawing her back to their problem. Steve's friend seemed in no hurry to escape the imminent danger. He slowly ducked his head behind the steering wheel. Then he came back up and said, "I was just wondering if you, like, were actually going to take me up on my offer of a getaway car or something. Or if I had to stay here for a while."

Steve laughed.

"Are you crazy?" she shouted first at Rhodes, then at Steve. "This is your rescue?"

Their assailants steadily advanced down the row of cars. Jane's grip on the bags tightened convulsively as the rear window of the Explorer shattered. She ducked her head and averted her eyes. Beads of glass flew into her hair and across the skin of her arms.

A bullet zinged and hit the truck, causing their rescuer to curse and disappear behind the door.

"How do I get over there?" Jane asked.

"Catch," Rhodes yelled.

Steve caught the gun and shot at the gunmen. "Go!"

She ran and jumped onto the tailgate of the truck, landing hard on her stomach and receiving a face full of dirt. The sounds of weapons firing, metal pings of bullets hitting cars, and a strange slow song on the radio surrounded her. Within moments Steve followed, pushing her toward the cab of the truck.

"Don't worry, lady—" Rhodes patted the dashboard "—she's got a Hemi."

Their knight in rusted armor slammed the ancient truck into gear and burned rubber from the parking lot. Tires squealed. Steve leaned over the tire well and aimed the gun but the kid kept his foot on the gas and left the Hispanic men behind.

She slid from side to side, her hair almost blinding her as it blew into her mouth and eyes. Straw and dirt blew into the air, choking her. She put her hand on the side of the pickup to pull herself to a sitting position.

"Stay down!" Steve shouted as he covered her head with his arm.

As they squealed through the next curve, she slid close to his side and he kept her there. But his eyes weren't concerned for her comfort. He slowly raised his head and searched the street behind them.

If anyone followed, they were left in the truck's dust. A "Hemi" must mean a fast, big engine. She'd have to read about them someday since she was grateful for their existence.

"So did you guys rob a store or something?" Rhodes asked through the back window while he directed the truck to the Interstate 35 on ramp and sped south.

"Always the clown. Get us out of here, Rhodes."

Steve sat with his back to the cab and helped her situate herself next to him. Thankfully, it was windy and noisy. She didn't need to discuss what had almost happened.

Death or capture. Rescue by a sexy dark-haired pirate with a dagger earring. It was too surreal for words.

STEVE BRACED HIS FOOT against the wheel hub as Rhodes darted in and out of traffic. He kept Jane's small body tucked into his side to keep her from sliding around the rusty truck bed. He stuck his new .45 in his waistband.

It was time to start thinking about their next step. He pulled a small pebble of glass from her hair just thankful Jane hadn't been shot.

"You can slow down, Rhodes. No reason to draw attention to ourselves since no one's following."

Rhodes eased off the gas and exited. A few minutes later they sat in front of a broken-down apartment building in a very poor neighborhood. It looked as if it should be condemned.

Rhodes slammed the truck door and grabbed the two bags from Jane's side. "Man, what did you guys do to piss off the *enojadizo* brothers?"

"You know who those punks are?" Steve asked.

"They tried to kill us," Jane said. "*Enojadizo* is Spanish for angry."

"I know, Jane." Steve tried to gently reminder her that they *both* spoke Spanish. No one grew up on a Texas ranch and worked undercover without knowing a bit of the language that was just beyond the border.

"Those guys are local guns for hire," Rhodes said. "You're lucky I got there in time."

"Just in the nick of time. Trying to be a hero?"

Rhodes cocked a smile. "Never been one before."

Local guns for hire. Whoever had framed Jane for murder knew he was helping her. The kidnappers were tired of playing games.

Steve kept Jane close to him. He knew what kind of work Rhodes did for the DEA. Deep undercover drug trafficking. So he didn't trust the neighborhood and barely trusted Rhodes. They walked up four flights of stairs and into a room with a simple doorknob lock.

"Sorry about the temporary accommodations, but I don't receive a huge housing allowance."

Jane took the bags and sat in the lone chair next to the folding TV tray.

"This is a hellhole, man." Steve shook Rhodes's hand and squeezed his shoulder, trying to convey how much he appreciated the rescue without saying it out loud. Not now. Not in front of Jane. She really seemed shaken up.

"Yeah. When you called this afternoon, I scrambled to find someplace for you. I'm still waiting to hear back. It's been a while, Woods. How ya been?"

"There's no computer here," Jane said without looking directly at either of them.

"Nope. A PC in this dump would mean I was an intellectual." He turned away from Jane and mouthed, "Is she all right?"

Steve shook his head. "Hey, man, could you bring a laptop to that place we're staying tonight? Did you manage the cash?"

"Cash is not a problem." Rhodes had his hand on the doorknob to leave.

"How about transportation?"

"Being taken care of," Rhodes said. "Did you eat?"

"Food would be great."

"Be right back."

The door shut quietly and he heard the thud of the bags slipping from Jane's lap to the floor.

"I don't believe this." Jane stood and went to the small, grimy window. "He doesn't have a computer?"

She had to understand he was doing the best he could. They were on the run, not undercover. This was totally different. He had no reference points, no experience, no place to start.

Bull, his starting point was Jane. She'd asked her Baltimore friend to confirm Rory was still alive. Steve needed to call and see if that had happened. Then he'd—they'd—get Rory back.

She was at her breaking point. A breaking point for Jane was only indicated by the slight rise in the pitch of her voice and the fact that she moved her arms while she spoke instead of hugging her middle.

"Keep it together, Janie. You can't lose it now."

Mothers in Jane's situation usually ranted. Not her. Or they shut down completely. But not his Janie. She tapped her foot as if she'd lost patience with him. She nervously nibbled on a fingernail until she noticed and then tucked her fingers in her front jeans pockets.

He was so proud of her for *not* losing it. For keeping everything together no matter how much he thought she *should* cave. Then he took a close look at the way she held her stomach—as if it hurt. A closer look at her face showed the stress in the taut lines around her eyes. The dark circles revealed more than a lack of sleep.

"I can tell you're shaken up. The first time you're caught in cross fire is a little hard on the nerves." He tried to divert the conversation away from Rory. They hadn't made much progress this afternoon, but he didn't want to verbalize that thought.

But then she didn't have to. No matter what her words indicated, she was thinking about her son. He waited until her eyes finally made direct contact with his and she stopped. Then like the Titanic hitting an iceberg, she sank.

Reaching out, he caught her around the waist and gently tugged her into his arms. Couldn't she let him in for a minute? Her heart beat as erratically as his own. And God, even after running and perspiring in fear, she smelled wonderful.

"It's okay, Janie." He smoothed her windblown curls. "We won't stop till we find Rory. Not ever."

Each word was a promise he meant to keep.

One resolute sniff and she pushed her stiff body back, totally under control again. He wanted to keep her wrapped against his chest. Wanted to shelter her from everything they were going through. He should tell her how he felt. Then maybe she'd open up and share some of those bottled emotions with him.

Instead, he shoved his hair back off his forehead, and repositioned his Stetson. The war with his conscience continued. Should they try this Jane's way? Or should he do what made sense to him—get a team working on obtaining the information they needed?

"Before you go any further, Steve, there's something you need to know about Rory's father."

"What?"

Rhodes knocked twice and came inside. Steve didn't enjoy the smile on his friend's face nor the interruption. Jane curled her arms around her stomach again and stared out the window.

"Hey, finally got a place for you to lie low tonight." He held up a bag. "I also have tacos."

Chapter Ten

The junkyard was the perfect ending to a terrible day. Jane shivered at the thought of what lived in the deepest, hidden parts of the old cars piled three or five high. The excessive humidity from the July afternoon had continued to build into a dank night. She swatted mosquitoes buzzing around her ears while picking her way along the path.

It was eleven-thirty, the clouds had gathered and the heavens were about to open up. The rain that had been their enemy at the lake was about to catch up with them again. Dark clouds were blowing their way, yet the air around them didn't seem to be moving at all.

"It's a camper. This is where we're staying?" she asked Rhodes. His nod verified her fear.

"A friend of mine uses this place. He'll crash at my pad tonight," the DEA agent said.

Was it a homeless person? Oh, God. She couldn't let her thoughts stray to Rory growing up…without parents, without love.

The derelict camper sat on tireless rims amidst rusting dishwashers, car parts and other discarded items. There was a three-foot dirt path around its edge and a tattered awning over the doorway.

A steel pole wedged in the middle of a large wooden spool covered in fast-food wrappers and crushed soda cans held up one side of the awning. The opposite was tied to junk on the far side of the path. A folding chair held together with more duct tape than original strap sat next to the door. She couldn't sit in that.

"I'll go get my laptop and wifi card from storage. The trailer is much better equipped than my company-issued apartment." He shook Steve's hand and headed up the path. "It'll take me a couple of hours to get back. Be safe."

"He's not taking his truck?"

"I talked him into leaving it here in case of an emergency." He jingled the keys, then shoved them in his front pocket.

The truck's engine smelled liked burning oil. In the confined space Rhodes's friend had carved out for his home, the odor overwhelmed all other possible foul aromas.

Jane set the bags down on the worn indoor-outdoor carpet that covered the dirt like a patio. Steve kept looking down the path after Rhodes.

"I might associate with a DEA undercover, but I'm still a bit paranoid. I need to check out where we are." He, too, disappeared into the cavern of precariously stacked junk.

Jane stood her ground and waited. The past few hours had become a steady blur of running and hiding. Desperation, fright and longing for Rory built inside her, crippling her thought process.

Not knowing what would come next was beginning to take a toll on her, too. She loved a well-ordered life and laboratory. Depended on it. The monotonous repetition of experiments kept her from thinking too much.

Sitting in the truck next to Steve, her mind had neared a meltdown. Or her body. Maybe both.

Or it might be the constant ache to tell Steve the truth about his son. Was it too late? How would he react? Whatever his reaction, he deserved to know the truth. It was easier not to assume how he'd react. But none of this tragedy had been easy.

Think of what needs to be done. Her mother's voice echoed

in her head. *Take it step-by-step. Logical progression by logical progression.*

Scooping up the bags, she entered the camper. She would make use of her time alone by reading the computer manuals they'd purchased. Then she'd be prepared to hack into the Maryland state records and track the person who forged the death certificate.

It might not be the person trying to frame her, but there should be some kind of a trail. Right? Wasn't there always a trail in the movies?

They needed to accomplish something toward finding Rory. Anything.

She wouldn't let herself doubt that they would find him. She had to believe Steve when he promised they wouldn't stop searching. They could do this. She had to believe in them both.

Okay, Jane, you're getting maudlin here. Get busy.

There wasn't much room in the travel trailer and she didn't see any bathroom. She turned the sink's tap, hoping for a drink, but rusty water barely trickled out so she quickly turned it off. There was a small table under the full-size, fold-down bed. They could rotate who slept—*if* they were here long enough to sleep.

Thank goodness she didn't have to share another bed with Steve. It didn't matter how big or small, she'd end up close, warm and completely enclosed in his arms. Now wasn't the time to mend fences. Nor imagine his hands moving up and down the length of her body. But it certainly didn't stop her from longing for it.

Or craving it like a sex-starved jailbird. Or a single mother who hadn't managed any level of intimacy since he'd ended the best six weeks of her life.

She had to act as if it didn't bother her. She tried to convince herself it didn't as she lifted the bed up into its travel position.

But each time it was harder and harder to pull free from

Steve's arms. Harder and harder to pretend to be strong. To stand on her own. Even before the kidnapping had brought Steve back into her life. She'd wanted to move her research to Dallas. Because she didn't want to be strong, emotionless and…alone?

Providing a stable life for her gifted son would require more than she could offer by herself. Her emotions had nothing to do with the logical choice of returning to where Rory's family lived.

The heavy manual made a thud on the table. There didn't seem to be any electricity in the trailer, but there was a battery-operated lantern. She opened the curtain behind her to let the light from a security lamp filter in, too, then turned the pages and burned another book into her memory.

She flipped the last page and closed her eyes, retrieving the volume from a shelf in her mind and opening the pages referring to system vulnerabilities, routers and packets. It was all there. Stuck away forever in a brain she feared would explode one day.

"Hey, that seat taken?" Steve asked as he slid onto the bench across from her. "I waited until you were finished… reading. That seems a strange word for what you do."

"I didn't hear you come inside." Her breath hitched when Steve squeezed his long legs into the tiny space under the table. The room seemed to get even smaller. "I think I can get the information we need."

"I never doubted it." He tipped his hat back off his forehead with one lean finger. It was a shot straight from any Western. His white teeth practically sparkled when the light caught them just right.

Think, think, think. Hacking…cracking…computers…

"There are always system vulnerabilities, and if you know how to exploit them, it's a breeze. You have to hit all the access points. The Internet goes through a lot of routers and machines—"

"Jane," he said, turning her monosyllabic name into a song. "I believe you, honey."

Good grief. Everything about him made her heart jump up and down. He didn't have to add an endearment. The sparkle of fun in his eyes made her breath catch again. His inviting grin was out of place for their situation. They should be thinking about Rory and only Rory.

Maybe he would if you told him he was Rory's father.

"I'd like to get started as soon as possible." She attempted to be all business. Working together was a temporary arrangement until they got Rory back. That was all. "Will Rhodes really be gone two hours?"

"He's on foot and has to make it across town."

Steve adjusted his legs under the cramped table so they no longer touched Jane. Her nerves were so tightly strung he could pluck them from across the room. And touching him only made her shift in her seat more. He shifted, too, but not because he wanted *less* of her body near him.

"Is something wrong?" she asked.

That was the question of the century. "What isn't wrong?"

"I'm a big girl. I think I can handle it."

"I think Hayden's our guy." That was genius. Just blurt it out. Just say her best friend wants her dead.

"You're delusional."

"Hear me out." He reached for her hands, but she quickly moved them into her lap. So he covered his movement by leaning forward over the table and linking his fingers together. "You contact him and a couple of hours later two goons show up trying to kill us."

"He couldn't possibly know goons like those men."

"They picked us up right after your call from the hotel." His voice treated Hayden like a suspect, making certain Jane knew. "I bet you told him we were headed to a mall, didn't you?"

Yes, she had. Her eyes couldn't hide the truth from him. Hayden was their guy. He needed to call his team.

"I don't believe you. Hayden wouldn't do that." She forced books back in her bag, stuffing them on the bench seat with her, then stood without touching anything. She looked like a brand-new colt ready to run to the hills at the slightest whisper.

"I want you to pull his bank records and see if there's been any unusual activity." *If* she could actually do that. *If* she could even locate what bank he used. There were so many small states up there, he might work in Maryland and live somewhere else.

"I'll do it, but it's not him." She straightened the edges of the bags. "I can't just sit here."

"We need to wait. Rhodes is a good guy. He'll be back with what you need."

She walked out anyway. Just as he reached the torn awning, the rain came down in sheets. Not a heavy drizzle or light rain. No, it was the flash flood kind of downpour this part of Texas was famous for. Steve couldn't see ten feet in front of him.

"Great. Wonderful." Jane dashed past him back into the trailer. "I need to find Rory and I'm stuck doing nothing."

Not a *we*, just an *I*.

She slammed her hand on the counter. He watched from outside on the makeshift porch even though water dripped on his shoulder. As much as he wanted to believe Jane could find the information they needed, he knew his team could find it faster.

He'd tried to think of a way to tell her, to ease her into the idea. But nothing came to mind. He was the straight-shooting guy on the team, the one who didn't pull any punches. He left the sensitivity classes to his partners. He wasn't much good at relationships. Never had been.

Except…yeah, except maybe when he'd met her. It didn't seem that either of them could do any wrong that go round.

This time it didn't seem fate would let anything happen right.

So he might as well hit her with the rest of his plan. He stayed outside the camper, getting wetter by the second. He spanned the doorway, filling the opening.

"I need to call Stubblefield," he said, trying not to plead like a groveling male who was wrong.

She spun around and stomped her foot, shaking the trailer. God, he was glad she didn't have a gun or it might have been blazing.

"No. Absolutely not." Her foot stomped the dirty linoleum again, her hands waved as if she was trying to shake something off and her voice trembled. "You can't contact the FBI."

"Selena Stubblefield helped us. Remember? They have access to information…and can get it easily. They can verify, if they haven't already, that Rory's alive and work to get him back. Don't you see? We need them and their resources. We can't do this on our own."

Inhaling a deep breath and slowly releasing it through her nose, she regained control of her actions. But he saw the resentment in her blue eyes.

Lightning flashed behind her and for a split second he could see her as a vengeful Valkyrie come to chop off his head. Her words echoed in the midst of the following thunder.

"I've given everything that's happened a lot of thought, too, Mr. FBI-aholic. I only know one thing for certain. Every time the FBI gets closer to me…I'm pushed further from my son."

Steve fell to the ground flat on his butt when Jane pushed his chest and ran from the camper into the rain.

"You're killing me," he mumbled to himself because she was completely out of sight.

They weren't secure here. Rain or no rain, he wasn't about to let her run around alone. He scrambled to his feet and followed her out into the downpour. Just around the first curve in the path she was stopped with her back to him.

"You ready to come back inside?" he roared over the noise of rain hitting the metal junk around them.

"Go away."

"I'm one of the good guys, remember?" He gently turned her to face him. It was crazy to be standing here in the rain discussing anything. "No matter what you might think right now."

Man, she looked good. No makeup, her hair plastered to her scalp, every part of her sopping wet and dripping. She didn't need to dress up to impress him. Shoot, she didn't need to dress at all. He could remember every inch of her body, wanting every inch of her body, loving every inch of her body. One look at her and he craved her more.

He missed their conversations. The long ones they had walking casually down by the pond. Or the short ones right before they couldn't stand it anymore and ripped their clothes off. He'd never connected with someone like that before.

Yep, she was great.

A simple description of the most complex human being he'd ever met.

After what she'd been through, he could wait in the rain if that was what she really wanted. Maybe she just needed to be away from him. No way that was going to happen. He was sticking to her side like permanent bond glue.

The rain was cool relief from the excessive humidity, but it came down in sheets and wasn't very pleasant to stand in. Jane blinked and rubbed the water from her eyes—her only reaction to the weather. He at least had his hat to protect his face. Shoot, standing here wasn't doing either of them any good. Only getting them wetter by the minute.

"Come on." He interlocked his fingers with hers. When she didn't pull away, he led her down the path and hurried to their shelter.

"Don't call the Bureau, Steve," she said the moment they

stepped through the door. Her lips quivered and her body shook.

Warmth. She needed warmth. The stress must be taking its toll on her. Wouldn't she understand why he needed to call when she was more in control of herself? He tossed his hat into the sink to drip dry, then went in search of a towel or blanket. He banged cabinet doors open and closed, finding one after another practically empty.

"Cap'n Crunch. Pop-Tarts. And a box of condoms." He slammed the last door shut not wanting to physically react to the sexy memories that just shot through his brain.

The small upright cupboard that served for a closet had some clothes tossed on the floor. He shoved his wet hair back from his face. "Guess laundry day hasn't happened in a while."

Jane stared into space, unsmiling, her hands rubbing her arms in an attempt to get warm. He could see the goose bumps from three feet away. Her vacant look started to worry him, so he pulled the outside door closed and locked it.

"Strip. Get out of those wet clothes before you... Shoot, I don't know. Are you going into shock, Dr. Palmer?" He pulled the curtain by the table.

"N-no."

"There's not one stupid thing in here that will dry you off." Dumping the clothes they'd bought that morning onto the cracked-vinyl seat, he picked up his extra shirt and began tousling her hair.

"Stop, you're going to break my neck."

"Then you do it."

While her hands were busy on top of her head, Steve bent down in the close space and removed her tennis shoes, tossing them to the opposite end of the camper.

"I'm not taking my clothes off," she managed between chattering teeth.

Looking up to answer her, he turned his head so his nose wouldn't be in her belly button. But he noticed her T-shirt stretched tight across her breasts. Her nipples strained through the material as if it wasn't there.

"You need to get warm." He swallowed hard, wondering how he'd managed to sound halfway in control. Especially after the images floating in his head just moments ago.

When he could force his body to do as it was told, he stood. His shoulders and chest bumped her abdomen on his way up. He snagged her and rubbed his hot hands up and down her frozen arms.

Yeah, he knew they were hot. His body was on fire. He couldn't stay this close to Jane for any length of time and not be. Two days next to her side had him churning like molten lava about to erupt from a frustrated volcano.

No matter what the circumstances, his body would know hers and hunger for her.

Okay. Yeah. Big deal. He was a grown man who could turn that area of his brain off. Right? Hadn't he done that for the past four years?

Shoot! Think about Jane. Her needs.

Not her possible needs.

"Sleeping...bag."

"Right. It's still in the truck." The door slammed behind Steve. Even the short thirty seconds opening the truck door, grabbing the sleeping bag and jumping back under the tarp had him drenched again before climbing the step to the camper.

It had to be more emotional turmoil than cold that had Jane's teeth chattering. She'd slowed so much, she didn't protest when he reached around her and untucked her shirt, pulling it up and over her head in one swift move. He kept his eyes firmly glued above her head, looking at a crack in the camper wall.

"Don't argue with me this time. Can you shuck your jeans or do I need to pull them off?" He moved his gaze to the button at the top of her zipper instead of the creamy skin his knuckles had just grazed.

Instead of her breasts that would fit perfectly in his hands. Instead of skimming his lips over—

"I can…do it." She pushed his hands away.

"Good. Fine." He avoided the urge to look at more of her and concentrated on the latch for the stowaway bed. Wondering how to move Jane out of the way without touching her. If he could just get past her. "I'll just get the sleeping bag."

Her jeans dropped and she caught herself before she fell. Yep, caught herself by falling into *him*. Her hands were like ice against his sizzling flesh.

God, he wanted her.

As quick as a cowboy escaping from a charging Brahma bull, he had her palms off him and at her sides. He might want her, but now wasn't the place or the time. Tiny thing that she was, he picked her up and set her on the small counter to get her out of his way.

A small yelp of surprise escaped, probably the shock of that wet, insignificant material called bikini underwear making closer contact with her skin. He wouldn't look. Nope, he needed to get that…

He couldn't remember because he was staring at every inch of her at once. And she stared at him. Her eyes locked on his and didn't let go.

Then she licked her lips.

Shoot. He swiped his hand over his face, blocking the vision of her sitting on that counter in a perfect place for him to warm her completely.

"Ah, Janie. Don't look at me that way." *Concentrate on the dang bed. The bed? No. The sleeping bag. Get the sleeping bag.*

"I'm not looking at you. I'm just cold."

Right.

Dropping the bed to its support, he unrolled the sleeping bag and kept his back to his patient. "You need to change your underwear before you get this wet."

"I am not—"

That suggestion got some fire in her blood. Maybe the key to getting her temperature up was to keep her mad at him.

"Come on. What are you afraid of? I've seen every part of you before."

Damn. That was *not* what he should have said.

The camper shook slightly when she jumped from the counter. She was going to pull off those skimpy panties just to prove she didn't fear him. Then he'd have to go against everything he wanted and ignore her delicious body because… because…

He heard her shifting, lifting one foot and then the other. Imagined the bikini-cut baby-blue satin panties—he'd looked at just about every package Walmart had—falling to the floor.

Shoot, there was a reason. He knew there was a good reason.

Scrubbing his face and pushing his hair back, he tried to think of every reason why taking her in his arms and kissing her senseless *wasn't* a good idea.

Number one, he'd be taking advantage. This was not a good place for rekindling a relationship.

But she'd be warm. Maybe as hot as him. So he wouldn't have to worry about her getting sick.

Number two, they didn't completely trust each other yet. He knew she was holding something back from him.

Okay, that was yesterday, but it still counted. Didn't it? Or had they gotten past that? Did she trust him?

Number three, he loved her.

Yeah. He'd never stopped loving her. *And this is a reason not to make love with her?*

"I need you…"

What?

"…to close your eyes, move to the side and let me get to my clothes."

Son of a… He was going nuts, but he did what she said. If he didn't, if he halfway lifted an eyelid and looked down…

He squeezed his eyes shut like a little kid, but the picture of her white smooth flesh was burned into the backs of his eyelids. There wasn't any way to get away from it. His heart beat a thousand miles per hour, and the comfort level in the front of his jeans dropped to nil.

The sleeping bag was tugged from his hand. The camper moved slightly again. He could tell she'd climbed to the farthest side of the bed. But he kept his eyes shut with his shoulders somehow pressed against the door. He must have backed up, but couldn't remember moving.

He was losing it. Big-time.

"You can open your eyes now."

"I don't think so."

He reached for the door, but fumbled with the lock. A psychological fumble or a real one due to the fact he couldn't see straight even with his eyes shut? He just needed out of there.

"Hold your racing horses just one minute."

"What?" he asked and turned around. Whoa, she wasn't completely covered. The skin of her shoulder was exposed, a slightly darker version of her derriere. And then there was her neck, and hands. Too much creamy skin.

Any skin had the same effect on him. He needed air.

Why was all the air suddenly sucked out of this camper?

"Aren't those wet clothes getting a little uncomfortable?" she asked. Her eyes held a glittery look at odds with her sultry voice.

"I'll be fine sitting outside." Outside where there was plenty of air since all the oxygen was gone inside the camper and he couldn't breathe. It wasn't his imagination. He really was laboring to suck air into his lungs. And the longer he looked at Jane, the harder it was to make anything move.

"Don't…please don't go, Steve."

"I, um, I have to. I'm not going to hurt you again, Janie."

"Stay?"

Low blow. She knew he wouldn't leave her alone if she

asked. And shoot, the second-hand vest was pressing on the shirt that *was* irritating his shoulders. Now he had to sit on the floor *and* stay wet.

Keeping his back to her, he sat and crossed his legs. His wet jeans made muddy streaks on the dirty linoleum as he folded and refolded himself into a comfortable position.

There was no comfortable position.

Chapter Eleven

It wasn't fair that he was so dang adorable.

And so terribly wrong. About everything.

Folding his semi-dry shirt under her head for a pillow, she curled into a ball to get warm and put the pretense of being angry aside.

I'm not going to hurt you again, Janie.

Hurt? Her father's 1968 version of *Webster's New Twentieth-Century Dictionary* stated the second definition as "to cause injury, loss or diminution to; to impair in value, quality, usefulness, beauty or pleasure; to injure; to damage; to harm."

Some people might think Steve had already hurt her. But she knew better. Her life hadn't shrunk or dwindled since Steve told her to go to Baltimore. It had grown with love for Rory. Grown better in quality, usefulness and beauty.

She thought of herself as a better person since Rory existed. All because of the love she and Steve had momentarily shared. As if he could read her thoughts and heard the word *love,* he shifted uncomfortably on the floor, straightening his legs, then pulling one up to his chest, as if uneasy to be in the same room with her.

That hadn't always been the case. In fact, according to that wind-up clock on the counter, it had only been true for the last forty-one hours and sixteen minutes. Their days together four years ago had been completely the opposite.

It didn't take a rocket scientist to notice that in spite of everything that had gone wrong in the past few days, Steve was still attracted to her. He might have had his eyes shut, but hers had seen how tight his jeans had gotten.

Warmth suddenly followed the tingle flowing through her body. It began at the top of her spine and seemed to spread to every nerve, then waved through her again.

She wasn't cold any longer.

Thinking about the weeks she'd spent with Steve spiked her temperature up several degrees. Her mind couldn't keep up with all the remembered sensations pouring into it. So she simply shut it down.

She wasn't going to think.

She was going to enjoy.

Not another thought to whether it was right or wrong.

Enjoy.

No consequences. Why not just live for the here…the now?

Steve shifted again.

"Oh, for goodness' sake, why don't you come up here and see if you can get comfortable?"

"I'll get everything wet."

"For a smart guy, sometimes you can be pretty dumb."

He craned his neck to look back at her. And yes, that what-are-you-talking-about look was there on his face.

"Good grief, Steve. *I'll* shut my eyes this time and you can change."

"I don't have any more jeans."

"So?"

"So? So?" He shoved his hand across his face and scraped a day's growth of beard with his nails.

That tingly need of desire shot through her again.

If there had been room in the small camper, he probably would have jumped to his feet and paced.

Thank God for small favors.

"I can control myself, Steve. Can't you?"

A blatant lie. She didn't want to control herself any longer.

She wanted him next to her. Wanted to draw comfort from the strength she felt in his arms. She wanted him. Period. Beyond any doubt. Assuredly, certainly, conclusively, decisively, enduringly. She listed the adverbs while waiting on his answer.

An answer that was taking much too much time.

"No."

Her heart smiled. She felt it move in her chest. He couldn't control himself.

"It's dangerous being this close to you. You're making me lose focus." He stood and rubbed his backside. "There's no way I'm getting into that bed with you while..."

She sat up and left the sleeping bag at her waist.

"While someone..." He spun on his boot heel and did an about-face. "For God's sake, Jane. Don't do that."

"I need you." She threw off the cover that was suddenly excruciatingly hot and slid her legs over the side of the bed.

"Come on, don't do this." He jerked farther away as she stood. "Two guys are gunning for us, the FBI is just a phone call away and we're in a broken-down camper surrounded on all sides by junk."

"Quit making excuses." She dragged a fingertip across the back of his neck and shook with the strong need that cascaded her senses. She hadn't felt this extraordinary feeling in such a very long time.

"I am not making excuses."

"Either you want me or you don't." This was real. She didn't care about where they were. "Steve, please?"

In the blink of an eye he had her by the shoulders, giving her a gentle shake, but no kiss. "You're making me crazy."

"Join the club." She needed to be flip. Keeping this on a casual level was a must. No pressure. No promises. "Be crazy now and sane after the rain ends."

She grabbed fistfuls of his wet shirt and gave a yank. Catching him off guard, she was able to bring his mouth to hers before he could object again. She needed him. He wanted her. So she'd enjoy. Take pleasure. Feel. Love.

Come alive in his arms.

Their noses collided and he didn't react. For two full seconds he just stared at her with eyes the size of ping-pong balls. His lips were closed tight and unyielding.

For two seconds.

Then he slanted his face to fit hers. And he kissed her as if there wasn't enough of her to go around. As if she was the last dessert ever to be served, and a thousand people were in line for leftovers. As if he wasn't sharing.

When he took a breath, she said, "You know there are more words for *crazy*."

"Besides *cuckoo, daft* and *wacky*," he said, giving her a brief, but luscious kiss between each word.

"Try *frenzied*."

Ripping the snaps of his shirt open, she tugged it over his shoulders to his elbows. His arms were pinned to his sides.

She returned the succulent, wet kisses he'd bestowed upon her. And no matter what he'd vowed just seconds before, he kissed her back. His hot hands held her at her middle and kept her from leaning into him, feeling all of him. She wanted more and would convince him he did, too.

"Unhinged."

She pulled on the shirt, bringing his bare chest and the rest of him intimately closer. With only her bra separating them, she felt his heart pound as loudly as hers.

It had been such a long time. She started toward his mouth again, but stopped at his flat nipples. Sucking and gently nipping the tips before she continued to reacquaint her lips with his body.

Her fingers skimmed his near-fatal bullet wound. The red puckered area made her want to cry, but not now. Now was about celebrating life, about being with the man she hungered for.

She was tempted to nuzzle his neck long enough to place

a visible love bite there, but too impatient to stop. She wanted him beyond the point of no return before she released him, but was dying for him to caress her. She already ached for him to stroke and touch her as only he could.

Knowing that he was sensitive behind his ears, she detoured there and tickled him with the tip of her tongue. Then blew gently across his wet skin and reveled in the knowledge that she caused his squirming.

"Quixotic," she whispered in that same ear, and nibbled on his neck. "Don't you love the sound of that one?" She nipped his skin and dropped soft kisses across his shoulder. "Instead of I'm crazy for you? I'm quixotic for you."

"Let go of my shirt and I'll show you quixotic." He was breathing hard. He could have broken free at any moment, but he let her decide when he'd be released. She was surprised that she was so calm. Excited yet deliberate and controlled.

The shirt dropped to the floor, forgotten as Steve wrapped her in his arms. His strength surrounded her as he lowered them to the edge of the bed, delivering soul-searching kisses the entire while.

"Any more examples?" he asked.

"Touched."

His hand seemed to float across her nonsexy sports bra. Somehow his touch made her feel like the sexiest woman of all time. All doubts were safely stowed away as she arched and filled his palm with her breast.

The interior of the camper drifted into darkness. The batteries must have run out on the lantern. The rain pounded on the nearby metal and matched the irregular tempo of Jane's blood racing through her veins.

Steve's hands slowed as if he were hesitant to continue. She wanted to reach out and stroke him so he'd join her eagerness. She twisted to her side, forcing him to his back. Her hands stumbled over his fly.

The wetness of the denim clung to his thighs as she

struggled to pull them down. And he was definitely not offering help. She saw his grin quickly turn to desire when she deliberately let her fingers drift across the cotton covering his swollen flesh.

He sucked in his breath and pushed at the heels of his boots, stuck under his jeans. Jane teetered between laughter and hunger. Each time he kicked at the material restraining him, his stomach and leg muscles contracted to lean, hard, rippling rock.

It was such a turn-on.

Muscles in general did nothing for her, but Steve's body... goodness.

He tried to sit up to get rid of the encumbrance his clothes caused, but Jane held up her hand to stop him. She sat straight and pulled the stretchy cotton from her body, freeing her breasts and causing another rapid inhale from Steve.

Scooting from his reach, she bent to remove the tangled mess his clothing had become.

"I could really get into this vocabulary thingy here, Dr. Palmer," he said, grinning with his hands behind his head, pulling his stomach and crunching his muscles.

Oh, my!

This time he lifted his hips when she tugged at the elastic waistband of his shorts. His grin disappeared when he sprang free of the material. Boxers finally gone. Jeans and boots on the floor. Any doubt she had about continuing disappeared. She needed Steve Woods.

"I have one last word, then no more talking."

She boldly straddled Steve and moved until her feminine mound rested firmly against his masculine one.

"Wild."

Wild was right.

Steve had tried his hardest to keep things under control. Kiss her and back off, that was his plan. Let her have her fun and maybe release some tension, but keep a lid on his own.

Until she'd touched him and he'd lost the battle. Now she'd climbed on top of him and he'd lost the war.

Jane moved against him, her readiness apparent. All he had to do was shift.

Shoot, he didn't want it like this. Their first time together again deserved romance and a real bed. He needed to tell her his feelings, right? He needed to say that he loved her. Didn't she want that?

Placing his hands on her hips, he stilled her movements. She was doing everything right and he was having a hard time remaining coherent. But he couldn't take advantage of her. She was emotionally overwrought even if she kept it suppressed beneath all that calm. She'd hate him afterward and he'd hate himself more.

And what about birth control? Yeah, there were condoms in the cabinet, but not *his* condoms. And he'd given up carrying one in his wallet a month after Jane had moved.

Jane was special to him. It was going to be difficult enough rebuilding a relationship with her. They didn't need any more complications.

"Stop thinking such bad thoughts or I might get a complex." She gently skimmed his forehead with her finger.

"I'm not thinking. That's the problem."

As she leaned forward, her nipples brushed his chest just enough to keep that "wild" thought in his brain. She poised long enough for her eyes to break contact with his and glance at his mouth.

Her kiss was hungry. Her sweet breasts flattened against him, his hands ached to stroke her until she was as crazy as him. But he planted them firmly on her hips, knowing if he moved he'd be beyond return.

"You're right," she said, moving against him again. "*You're* not thinking about this. Am I doing something wrong?"

"No! No. It's—"

"Don't think about anything, Steve. I don't want any commitment from you. I just, well, I need this. I want you." She sat up again and wrapped her fingers around him.

Whoa. He wouldn't lose his reasoning ability and give in. This was more important than…than gratification.

There *were* consequences. He couldn't for the life of him think what they were, but he knew there were. He remembered that much.

Stilling her caress, he began an exploration of his own. She needed release, so he'd give it to her. His fingers fondled and stroked between her legs. She rocked against him.

Sexy sighs escaped her lips. Her moans shot him back to the long nights of lovemaking they'd shared. Hours and hours of pleasure-filled sighs of genuine love. He'd been such a fool to let her go.

Consequences be damned.

Unable to stand it any longer, he flipped her under him and entered her sleekness. She was hot and ready and unbelievable. He drew a ragged breath, shuddering with anticipation.

How could he have lived without Jane for almost four years?

Passion at its purest sent shivers up his spine. His body responded, wanting to drive into her as if there wasn't a tomorrow.

He had to slow down, take his time, make this last. He kissed her—long and deep, with as much love as he could. Sharing a moment out of time that he'd thought lost.

Jane's arms went around his neck, pulling him closer. Her all-knowing smile told him she'd accepted his unconditional surrender. He sank farther into her warmth and never wanted to leave. He couldn't get enough of her. Not by a long shot. He'd never get enough of her.

Ever.

He nuzzled her neck with his lips. Placed sumptuous kisses to every part of her body within his reach. He watched the gentle sway of her breasts as he thrust.

Powerless to set aside the temptation, he laved them with

his mouth. First caressing the soft peaks and then the supple sides. He loved the perfect fit of them in the palm of his hand.

Lowering his face to hers, she stared into his eyes. Her short practical nails scraped his scalp as she ferociously pulled his lips into a kiss that ceased his breathing.

Seconds passed as he quenched his craving. He must have slowed their pace because she whimpered and ground her hips into his.

Wanting more.

Demanding more.

Rain continued to pour, and the trailer rocked under them, as he loved her like nothing had changed. As if his telling her to go hadn't kept them apart.

Between their bodies, the heat built and raged hot enough to melt steel. She tightened, and he increased their rhythm to push her over the edge.

The volcano that simmered inside him finally erupted. Jane squeezed again and drew every drop of energy from his body.

He dropped his forehead to hers. Her warm breath drifted by his ear reminding him how everything had started, making him want to begin again as soon as he could breathe. He must be crushing her, but moving just wasn't an option.

She lifted his face, turning him to meet her mouth. Another soul-exploding kiss and he didn't want to separate at all. As his breathing became less ragged and the roaring subsided in his ears, he heard the muted beeping of a phone.

"Jane, I think we need to get something straight."

The phone beeped, then played the irritating beep again.

"Shoot. That must be Rhodes."

"Hurry." She shoved at his shoulders and he hesitantly rolled off the bed. "The phone's under the clothes you dumped on the bench."

All chances of discussing what had just happened between them were gone. He finally located the cell phone. "Yeah?"

"I got everything and should be there in ten minutes."

"See you in a few." Steve disconnected.

Jane was already pulling on her clothes.

Chapter Twelve

"We really need to talk about what just happened." He reached for his boxers and dry shirt. God, he knew he'd hate himself. He should have kept tighter control on his fly.

"No, we don't. It was…nothing." She shrugged and had her jeans up around her hips and was reaching for her T-shirt before he could blink.

"Really?" He shoved his fists through the armholes. He'd seen her face as she'd come apart in his arms. Neither of them had just experienced "nothing." It was the real thing and she was avoiding it like the plague.

"We need to find Rory." She pulled the wet shirt over her head without flinching.

"We need to call the Bureau." He would not grimace at the wet, cold jeans. No way would he react. She hadn't. He wouldn't. Shoot, he hated wet jeans.

"I can get the information we need, Steve. You asked me to trust you. Now I'm asking the same."

"We've wasted enough time today. We haven't accomplished a thing." He sat on the thin mattress and pulled on his boots.

Jane closed her eyes. She took a deep breath and slowly released it. He was aware of her actions and then realized exactly what he'd said. The words had to have hurt her feelings. They'd just made love. She had to be hurt, but gave away nothing. She had complete control over any emotion a normal person would have shown.

"I've got to try. I can't live with myself if I don't." She reached under the table—right between his legs without any comment—to pull free the bag she'd brought. "Your friends didn't believe me before. What makes you think they will now?"

A spark of anger. He saw it. Recognized it. But just as quick as a campfire ember covered by a northern wind, her spark was snuffed out.

"I'm sure they've already spoken to Hayden. We need to find out."

"I won't discuss it." That blank emotional curtain was back in place.

"Blast it, Jane. Get mad at me, at the kidnappers, at some-body. Yell. Scream. Kick the wall. Do something. Talk to me about what just happened between us."

"Making a spectacle of myself by yelling or acting out won't do anyone any good." She turned the lock. "I trust what my parents strived to teach me about keeping a calm, rational mind in a crisis."

"You asked why the guys at the Bureau didn't believe you." His words made her stop, her hand on the doorknob, her back to him. "Your emotionless nonreactions sealed your coffin, sweetheart. Acting like a Vulcan had everyone convinced you were lying."

Stupid.

Her shoulders slumped forward and a short dismaying breath escaped. He was an absolute idiot. She couldn't hide the hurt and didn't believe he wasn't included in that "every-one." Before he could explain, she threw those same shoulders back, hugged the bag to her chest and stepped outside.

He banged the bed back to its stowaway position, threw the sleeping bag to the other end of the camper and raised the blind to watch Jane sit in the duct-tape chair.

A motorcycle pulled up behind the truck. The driver tapped

the horn twice, signaling it was Rhodes. The bike had hard-side saddlebags, making it easy to keep a laptop out of the rain.

God, he was losing the edge that had him doing this job and had kept him alive for ten years. If it had been someone else threatening Jane or those two crazy brothers... His gun was somewhere under the table. Jane would be dead. He might be dead. Rory would be lost.

He crawled from under the cramped table just in time to back into Jane. She held a laptop the size of a suitcase in her arms and gestured that she wanted to get by.

So they weren't going to talk. He needed to call Stubblefield and wanted Jane's okay. Not her permission, just a reluctant agreement that it was the right thing to do. But he didn't want a full-blown argument. Shoot, maybe he did, but it wasn't going to happen.

He left the trailer and leaned on a pile of junk just within view. Rhodes had run an extension cord from the outlet on the light pole so Jane could run the laptop longer without using the battery. Then he disappeared in the junk.

With her wet hair quickly braided to stay out of the way, she leaned back and stretched on the bench. He was drenched again from the top of his Stetson to the tips of his boots, but he couldn't stop watching her.

Sitting there acting as if nothing was wrong. As if they hadn't just argued. As if she hadn't been pissed at him three minutes after they'd made love.

But she was. He'd seen it in her eyes. The Valkyrie hadn't left. Jane was barely subdued under that ironclad determination *not* to show emotion. Jane's fingers began flying across the keys. All after fifteen minutes of flipping pages. Her version of reading.

That amazed him. Her brain. And to think that her son may have her gift. She'd called it a photographic memory for lack of a better term. Millions of pages of information stored away in her gray matter—instant and total recall with the blink of an eye.

And yet she was still so naive.

With Jane safely planted in front of the computer, he turned back down the path, his boots now sloshing through the mud.

"I'm right about calling the Bureau!" he yelled into the storm.

She can't hear you. And you are an idiot. He could have done something to convince her he was right. They needed the FBI and cops on their side. Ten years experience amounted to something. Didn't it?

It would take someone with more than a photographic memory to break into protected state records. He knew a little about systems, too. A hacker with a lot of experience could eventually gain enough pieces of the puzzle through trial and error. But it would take a long time without that experience to find a forged death certificate.

They simply didn't have the time.

Close by, he found an overhang with enough protection to get his face out of the rain. Water poured off his hat as he dipped his head to retrieve the number from his wallet. He stared at the one picture of Jane he'd kept with him the past four years. A black-and-white snapshot from a photo booth out at Valley View Mall.

For a brief moment he imagined covering it with a picture of Jane with her son. He hesitated punching in his former partner's number, but it was the right thing to do. Before they could do anything, they needed information—on Jane's friends, an ID on who forged Rory's death certificate, forensics from the murder scene. If any of the Brant ransom had turned up, that could lead them to the kidnappers.

But no ransom note was a bad sign. If it weren't for the attempt to frame Jane, it would be Bobby Joe Hill in the third grade all over again. Missing without a trace.

Not Jane's son.

As brilliant as Jane was, she couldn't hack into all those systems by herself as fast as they needed. Or trace where the suspect might currently be headed. They needed information two days ago.

And he didn't like Jane being shot at, either. What if George or Windstrom or McCaffrey had found them? He'd never have fired his weapon. But could he say the same for his colleagues?

He couldn't do this alone.

And Jane would never surrender herself. He saw that look of defiance in her eyes.

His only option was to glean information from Stubblefield.

Convincing himself he had to make the call, Steve punched Talk. The line stopped ringing, but no one spoke. Damn rain caused all kinds of inconveniences and bad connections. No tellin' when the storm would pass.

"Stubblefield, can you hear me?"

"Steve. You called." It didn't particularly sound like Selena was thrilled to hear from him. "The death certificate was forged. We sent an agent to interview Jane's friends. The boy's alive."

"It's about time," he said, relieved. That meant the team was working on the case. They'd find Rory.

"We followed procedure."

"I don't care whose head rolls later, Stubblefield. All I want right now—"

"Where are you?"

"We're…safe." Something held him back. His gut reaction told him to keep his location to himself. He couldn't take another chance with Jane's life. "We need to come in."

"No. No, you can't."

"Why not? Why the hesitation?" If they knew Rory was alive, then evading the FBI could eventually be worked out. He might be suspended, but Jane wouldn't have men shooting at her anymore.

"Steve? Steve, are you there?"

He moved until the phone had less crackling on the line. "I said why can't we come in?"

Water seeped through his jeans. He was more than ready for a dry set of clothes. More than ready for something to go their way. More than ready to find Jane's son.

"We've accessed Hayden Hughes's e-mail." *Yes.* "He's hired a hit on Jane. We think he's behind the kidnappings."

"There were two goons at the mall."

"It'll be better for you to go straight to a safe house," she said.

"I need to be a part of this, Stubblefield." He couldn't just walk away. "God, it's her son."

"Everyone's working on it. We both know what your primary concern should be, and that's to keep Dr. Palmer safe. Especially if you won't tell me where you are."

"That's not an option." So he was paranoid. Better safe than sorry, right?

"I could set you up in a hotel here in San Antonio, but I don't think you want that." She paused and the line crackled more. "Remember how to get to that place just west of town? It's still a safe house. Do you have your cell? I could call with updates."

The hair rose on the back of his neck despite being plastered by rain. That gut instinct that had worked for him for so long kicked him a couple of times.

Cells were just too easy to trace. Had he screwed up by calling? Didn't he trust them? His friends. His coworkers. The people he'd fought crime with on a daily basis for the past ten years.

For himself…yes. But for Rory and Jane?

"I'll call you when Jane's safe." In fact, he'd been on the line long enough. He disconnected. He slid the prepaid phone into his wet back pocket. Better than drowning it in the rain that was still coming down in buckets.

One step in the direction of the trailer had him nose-to-nose with Rhodes. "Got a minute? I went to the office and grabbed us some cold ones."

They just stood there. Steve's hat created a gutter for the water to flow straight down his back. Rhodes's yellow rain gear didn't protect his face with the wind blowing in every direction. His friend had gotten a bit older, but hid it well.

"Dude, what were you thinking?" Steve asked. Thunder crackled in the far distance, barely audible above the rain pouring down on the rusty castoffs of the junkyard. "You brought a classic 1967 Ford to a gun fight."

They moved under the awning and both wiped the water from their faces.

"Not my choice, man. She's my only car that holds more than two. Want a beer?" He handed him a can and pushed the rain hood off his head. "I borrowed them from the owner's stash."

"Last assignment they had me in a beige Volvo." They both popped the tops.

"You told the lovely Jane I'm DEA. Probably blew my cover."

"Sorry I sucked you into this, Rhodes, but I didn't have a choice."

"Not a real problem. I'm ready to get out anyway." Rhodes shrugged. "She's cool, you know, for a genius."

"They framed her for murder. Stole her son. And she's trying to do the work required of an experienced intelligence team."

"And yet she keeps on going," Rhodes said. "I want to finish this assignment. You'll keep my part out of this with your boss?"

"You got it."

"One call and you can retrieve the information you need. Why waste time trying to breach the firewall?"

"It's complicated." Steve wiped the moisture from his face. At least the rain hid the sudden sweat that covered his upper lip. Something settled wrong in his gut. The feeling that he needed to get Jane away from here wouldn't leave him alone.

"Say the word and I'll pull out with you."

"I can't let you do that, man." Steve admired Rhodes's loyalty. "One of us losing his job is enough."

Through the window, they watched Jane work. Her concentration remained focused on the computer screen.

"She's hiding something," Rhodes stated out of the blue. The undercover agent finished his beer and Steve had barely sipped his.

"Yeah." He turned his can up and gulped. "What do you want for the truck?"

"You know how it works, Woods." Rhodes tipped his bottle in a mock salute. "There may be a day when you'll answer the phone and can't ask any questions."

ONE CLOSE LIGHTNING BURST and everything Jane had accomplished in the past hour would be for nothing. The broadband card Rhodes had brought was keeping its connection, but how long would it last? It was safer to shut the laptop down. But what if the storm didn't pass for a couple of hours?

No, she had to keep working. Each step brought her closer to her son's kidnapper. And closure with Steve.

Their lovemaking was a comforting interlude between old friends. Nothing more. They were two people who needed a few minutes to forget their worries. No matter how much she desired a relationship with Steve, she wouldn't make anything more of it.

But making love with him had been so wonderfully right. To be in his arms again…it was magical. It had taken all the control she could gather to say it had meant nothing. Maybe he'd seen straight through her. Maybe he wanted more?

She was lying to herself. Steve Woods was a man committed to his career and she happened to be a part of that work. For now.

She heard someone at the door and knew it was Steve. The sound of his boots scraping the floor confirmed it.

"We have to talk, Jane."

Hat in hand, drips adding to the puddle at his feet, he wavered. The brim circled through his hands again. Strong hands. Gentle hands.

He was nervous. What could possibly have happened now? She didn't want to know. Not really. Nothing would change her mind. Leaving before she discovered exactly what the FBI knew about Rory wasn't an option.

"You called your team." Hating the thoughts that came to her, she asked, "Did something happen to Rory?"

"God, no. They haven't found him yet, but they will. They know he's been kidnapped and everyone's working round the clock." He tortured the brim of that hat while she caught her breath. "I'm sorry I scared you. I didn't know how you'd take finding out that... Shoot, there's only one way to say it. Stubblefield told me they connected Hayden to the kidnapping."

A choking tightness crushed her chest.

Shut the emotion off. It only gets in the way, Jane. Her parents were right.

Steve had told her he would call his colleagues. Her mind logically accepted that he would. But she'd stupidly let her heart cling to the hope that he'd believe in her. Trust her. Hadn't they just shared...?

What? She'd just spent the past hour trying to convince herself they were just old friends. Maybe they weren't even that. No matter how much she wanted something different, she had to accept facts.

"Did you hear me? Stubblefield told me Hayden hired the men who tried to kill you at the mall."

Emotions get in the way, Jane. They always muddy logical thought. The consequences are always too high. Don't let anything come between you and the task at hand.

"I heard and I don't believe you. The FBI's information hasn't been reliable so far. We need the information I'm decrypting to find Rory no matter who kidnapped him. We can argue later."

"You really found something?"

"A file that's received priority activity in the Dallas Bureau."

"Where?"

"You wanted to know what your team had discovered. So I took a look." She tried to sound casual. *Don't let anything come between you and the task at hand.* "I'm not leaving until I know what this file contains."

"You hacked into the FBI?"

"*Hack* isn't the right word. I used your password and gained access to the program they were running. Don't look so surprised." Yet he was. He *had* doubted her ability. "Most people use a name they won't forget. So I tried your friend's name, the one that disappeared, and then remembered *The Hitchhiker's Guide to the Galaxy.* Zaphod was one of your favorite characters."

He looked at her as if she was a real alien hitchhiking across Texas.

"I told you to trust me, Steve. Discovering your password was a series of logical steps. It took someone who knows you, not a genius." She shook her head. She had to be imagining his look of admiration.

"I could have given you my password. I honestly thought I'd be locked out by now. What did you find?" he finally asked.

"Agent McCaffrey authorized an internal search." Focusing on the screen still didn't help her ignore the churning in her stomach. *Ignore Steve, talk about the FBI agent.* "I haven't identified the originator or who recently deleted the file."

But she would. They weren't leaving until she was finished.

"If they're rushing, it probably does have something to do with Rory. You'd make a heck of an agent, Janie. You're performing under duress as well as most of my team does on a difficult day."

She could be snide about his team's performance, but the words were a high compliment from Steve. He had every faith in his team. A team of experts who performed above and beyond, time after time.

So why the mistakes this go around?

Pretending to look at the rolling information on the laptop, she was able to catch glimpses of Steve's reflection. She expected him to begin pacing, but it seemed the nervous habit had been replaced with crunching the edge of his hat.

"When did you figure out Hayden was involved?" he asked.

"I didn't." It was hard to swallow again.

"But you're so calm about it." Steve leaned a little too close, trying to see the screen, and dripped water on her shoulder. He took a step back.

"I learned not to let problems or emotions distract me." What could she say? How could she explain in a moment all the years of training her mother had put her through? "Your team discovered the death certificate was falsified this afternoon. That's what instigated the internal search."

He continued to torture the hat and stare at her.

"But you were right. Given time, they did discover their mistake." She wanted to make amends for their earlier argument. How did one sincerely apologize? "Should I assume you're ready to head back to your team?"

"Not exactly. I want to take you to a safe house. Rhodes has agreed to stay with you while I head back to the Bureau."

"But I can help."

"I know you can."

She could live without honesty from Steve. But she couldn't stand by and let him stick her in a safe house, keeping her away from the search. She could ditch the DEA agent. And then what?

"I have to do something, Steve. I'll go crazy just sitting around."

"They'll make me do the same thing. Probably from a holding cell." He placed his hat back on his head. "We have to leave."

"I won't stop looking for Rory."

Don't let anything come between you and the task at hand.

Maybe her mother had meant more with this advice than just the job. Maybe she'd meant life.

If this program would finish, it would end the arguing. They'd have answers. She didn't know what rambled around inside that gorgeous head of Steve's and wouldn't if she kept to her parents' advice of staying centered on one task. She needed a balance to her life. Come to think about it, her parents hadn't adhered to the logic they'd preached.

Her family had moved time after time, following their hearts, trying to protect her. She'd come back to Dallas to break a cycle. She couldn't change anything by continuing to ignore the truth. She had to admit the truth about Rory and deal with the consequences.

It was time to tell Steve he was Rory's father.

"Steve, I've wanted to explain—"

"Jane, we can't ignore—"

They spoke at once and she turned on the narrow bench to face him. "Go ahead." He put that silly hat into the sink and pressed his lips together time and again instead of speaking. But it was easier to let him start.

"In normal circumstances, I'd probably let you talk first. But there's nothing normal about you." He scratched his forehead, then stuffed his hands into his pockets. "You—we can't ignore what happened this afternoon."

"There's something much bigger that I need to speak to you about."

"Now see, you can't say something like that and expect

a person as intimidated as me not to stop talking and just listen."

"Intimidated?" She searched his face. He was serious. "You are the least intimidated person I've ever met."

"Not around you, hon." He scrubbed his face with his hand and ended by pinching the bridge of his nose. A sign to her that he was about to pace, but the small trailer didn't allow for the action. "No matter what you say out loud, we weren't just two friends relieving tension this afternoon."

"You made me feel alive again, but I didn't want you to feel obligated."

Two steps and he sat next to her, his body twisted in the seat to face her. She shoved the laptop toward the front window, away from them.

"I've been 'obligated' since I first saw you on the UTA campus." He covered her hands with his. "Four years ago."

Did he already know about Rory? Was he opening the conversation so she could tell him the truth? "I've wanted to tell you, but something always went wrong and then he was kidnapped and you didn't believe me."

"Take a deep breath, sweetheart." He placed a hand on her shoulder. "What are you talking about?"

He didn't know. There was concern in his look, not agitation, not disappointment. Nothing to indicate he knew she'd been lying. So she was back to determining how to tell a man he was a father and at the same time state that his son had been kidnapped.

"We're both agreed that there's more between us than just sex." He replaced his hand over hers. "Right?"

She felt his warmth, but more. The strength of him and his unwavering confidence in her was transferred through his hold like a direct stream of energy. No matter what, she had to tell him he was fighting for his son.

"Steve, Rory is—"

His mouth sealed the truth from escaping her lips. She

couldn't lose her senses this time. She had to tell him the truth.

Rhodes pulled the door open. "I hate to interrupt your... um, discussion, but we have company."

The door bounced open, not catching behind Rhodes, who now ran across the open area toward the truck.

"How much longer?" Steve asked her.

"I'm not certain. The encryption isn't very complicated. Minutes or hours." His hand slipped from hers. "Steve, I have to tell you—"

"Take the laptop and hide under the table. And for God's sake, Jane. This time listen to me."

Chapter Thirteen

Jane shoved the open laptop into the cabinet, ignoring Steve's command to listen and obey. She couldn't stay protected in the camper while the father of her child risked his life again. She had to help.

Careful to keep the wind from slamming the door or draw Steve's attention, she eased her way to the outdoor carpet. The mercury light atop the pole pushed the darkness to the edge of the clearing, giving an advantage to anyone hiding in the depths of junk. One blink she and Steve were alone and the next, two huge men in black dove at him.

The three men fell into Rhodes's motorcycle, knocking it to the ground. The helmet rolled toward the folding chair to her left, as the world suddenly became a series of grunts and oofs. She was unable to move, her feet frozen, not knowing how to help.

Why didn't Rhodes jump in and get rid of these monsters?

Steve's body cracked across the bike as one of the men slammed him backward. There were words in Spanish she couldn't completely catch. The familiar smell of cheap aftershave invaded her nose—the *enojadizo* brothers. How did they find them?

A thick arm grabbed her around the waist and her feet were lifted off the ground. She cried out and Steve's head snapped in her direction as a second man punched him in the face...hard.

She couldn't follow her instincts and scream. It would distract Steve. She struggled, squirming in the man's grasp, attempting to slip through his grip. Wrapping her ankles around his shins, she tangled his feet as he tried to carry her toward the dark. She succeeded in tripping the man to the muddy ground.

None of the self-defense techniques she'd memorized worked to get her free from the massive man. Sitting across her back, he pinned her to the ground with his weight, ignoring her insignificant attempts to get away. She needed something...

Rhodes's motorcycle helmet had rolled inches beyond her reach. She pushed her feet against the step of the camper. Shoving with all her might, stretching, her fingers just brushed the cool plastic.

"No tan de prisa!"

Not so fast? She could barely twist enough to see that the man holding her pointed a gun in Steve's direction. God help her, less than an inch to the helmet.

As hard as he tried, he couldn't get to her. Fury surged through Steve as he watched Jane pinned to the ground by a third man pointing a handgun in his direction. Gun Guy was trying to get a bead on him.

Steve scrambled to his feet and grabbed for his weapon at the hollow of his back. Damn! No gun. He'd lost it during the struggle. Steve exchanged punches with the man as the other tried to grab him from behind, giving him the perfect target for an elbow strike to the nose. Blood spurted as the man dropped to the ground. Steve caught a glimpse of him scrambling toward their pickup as his second assailant pulled a knife and sliced it through the air in his direction. Knife Guy was between him and Jane but also provided cover from the handgun.

"Come on, now. Is that really playing fair?" Steve spun

around, aiming his foot at the knife, but caught the side of his opponent's head instead. At least he'd connected with something.

"I don't care how much for you alive," Knife Guy growled in heavily accented English while wiping blood from his ear. "I will hurt you bad. You're *muerto*."

He pitched his body forward and sliced the air twice, causing Steve to hop backward. The third time, Steve wasn't as fast and the knife slashed his arm.

"Son of a…" Ignoring the pain, Steve backed up looking for anything to ward off the switchblade as Knife Guy came at him again. Nothing.

In the middle of a junkyard with nothing to swing.

Careful to keep Knife Guy between him and the weapon pointed in his direction, he ripped his shirt off and wrapped it around his left wrist. He blocked the next swipe with his wrapped arm and followed through with a roundhouse punch to the man's face. Not willing to give up his advantage, he continued his attack with a knee strike to the groin. The knife flew to the ground but clattered under a doorless refrigerator.

"Where's your partner?" Steve searched the darkness and caught sight of Runt Guy pinned to the ground by Rhodes next to the truck.

"No!" Jane screamed from the other side of the clearing as a wild shot burst through the worn tarp above her head.

He didn't have time to look for his gun as he turned toward Jane and saw her roll over and strike her assailant with a motorcycle helmet, sending the man off her back as the gun flew in the opposite direction. She scrambled forward on her hands and knees.

As Steve went for the gun, Knifeless Guy's shoulder shoved into his side. He hadn't seen the running tackle coming, but he grabbed on to the man and pulled him across the ground with him.

The man reached for Steve's neck, strangling him as he sneered in his face. Steve grabbed at anything but only came up with mud. Taking a fistful of the thick gooey substance, he shoved it up the man's nose with an open palm strike. The force of the blow sent the man reeling backward.

Steve jumped to his feet as Knifeless Guy rolled and attempted to stand. He thrust the toe of his boot into the man's stomach hard enough to make him curl into a fetal position. Another kick to the kidney had him whimpering like a baby. He wasn't moving, but was groaning in agony.

Steve turned to help Jane just as another shot rang out.

"I missed him. He's running," Jane shouted. Her hands shook from the recoil as she pointed the gun down the path after Gun Guy.

"Jane, shoot him if he moves."

Redirecting the barrel of the gun to her new target, Jane looked more than capable of finishing the job. Her confidence bolstered Steve to charge down the path after Gun Guy. He heard the perp hitting junk in front of him. He had to catch him. Rory's life depended on it. The worn soles of his boots slid in the mud, but he had an advantage over his target. He knew the layout of the junkyard from his earlier exploration. Gaining on the man, Steve made an airborne leap, slamming the bastard headfirst into an open car door. He landed on top of him, prepared to do battle.

No movement.

Limp.

He grabbed a handful of the guy's T-shirt and pulled him back to the camper.

"Heads up." Rhodes tossed him a roll of duct tape.

"He's out cold." Steve pulled the man's hands together and used the tape to secure his wrists. He frisked the unconscious third man. "Nothing."

"Sorry to be late to the party," Rhodes said. "Little brother there got a jump on my head." He rubbed the back of his neck. "I'm not sure who might have heard the shots. The cops might be here soon."

"We can't leave yet," Steve said. "We need information."

"It ain't coming from my guy, he's out cold." Rhodes looked at the man they were dragging through the mud. "Guess this one's out for a while, too."

Knifeless Guy was still rolling on the ground holding his gut. Jane's hands shook as she took deep breaths and blew out through her mouth. She would have herself under control in a minute.

"You okay?" he asked.

A little nod.

God, she was brave. Strong. Capable. And he wanted nothing more than to take her in his arms and love her for the rest of his life. This was a Jane he'd never seen, one he hadn't counted on, but could from this moment forward.

"Let's find out what this guy knows," Steve said, gently prying the gun from her fingers.

"My God, Steve. You're bleeding." Jane took his arm and used the bottom of her shirt to wipe some of the blood away. "You're going to need stitches."

"I'm fine." Ignoring his injury, he pulled the man off the ground and tossed him on the folding chair. "Tape him."

Rhodes took the tape and used it generously on Knifeless Guy's hands and feet, then searched his pockets.

"Cell phone," Rhodes said. "The call history has been erased."

"Are we doing things the easy way or do I need to send my girlfriend into the trailer so she won't get sick?" Steve let himself sound a little crazy. This wasn't a typical interrogation, he couldn't use ordinary techniques. "What's your name?" he demanded as he pointed the gun at his face.

The man grunted. Steve walked behind the chair.

Jane took the roll of tape from a makeshift table and bound Steve's knife wound. "That should hold until you get to a hospital. I'll be in the camper," she said, opening the door. "I'd rather not be sick."

Steve wrapped his arm around the man's neck and pushed the barrel of his weapon up the guy's nostril. "Look, man, the way I see it, I have two choices. I can call the authorities and tell them where you are, but that doesn't get me anything I need. Or you can tell me who hired you and I won't pierce your nose."

The guy tried to get away, but succeeded in knocking himself over as Steve relaxed his hold.

Good.

"Who hired you? Where were you supposed to take us?" Steve looked the man in the eye, then yanked him upright again. He kept his voice low, but loud enough so the man knew he meant business.

"I don't have time for games. Now tell me who hired you before I lose my cool and pull this trigger."

Jane tried unsuccessfully not to watch or listen to what was happening outside through the window. Tried not to pay attention to Steve. A Steve she had never seen before. A Steve who had a gun in one hand and an attempted murderer in the other.

The man who Rhodes had knocked unconscious was awake and staring at Steve with huge frightened eyes. She didn't care. She *wouldn't* care. These men had tried to kill them and were involved in the disappearance of her son. She wouldn't allow herself to care. No matter what Steve did, she wouldn't interfere.

"The number's in my phone, man," the guy in the chair said, caving in. "I was supposed to text when we got you. That's it."

"Don't give me that crap," Steve shouted. "Where were you supposed to take us?"

"Esta en el caro. Por favor no nos maten," the little guy shouted from the ground.

"What kind of car?" Rhodes asked. "What street?"

The man must have answered because Rhodes took off at a gallop, but Jane couldn't hear. She let the curtain fall. One way not to care was not to watch.

The decryption program should be done. Every instinct

she had told her the file was important. She would discover what secrets it held and then tell Steve her own. Time was up. Steve needed to know he was searching for his son.

"Do you know how amazing it is to see you sitting here, covered in mud but without a scratch after what we've just been through?"

When had he slipped into the camper? She looked up at him and in one rough, exciting move his hand slid up and around her neck to bring her closer. His kiss was hard and slashed across her mouth, making her think of raw, pure sex. He didn't back off and tilted her head back, demanding a response. She gave it.

Her arms wound around his waist and up his back, pulling every sensitive part of her against him. They were alive and in each other's arms. Nothing else mattered except Rory.

The tension of the past two days worked its way into their frenzied movements. She pushed everything from her mind and enjoyed the complete feeling of his lips.

As quickly as their passion ignited, they were back under control. The need was still there—plain in the ache shadowing his eyes. He gently released her and she sat on the worn cushion.

"We can't wait on you to finish," Steve said. "Time to go."

The screen changed. The program silently announced it was complete. She'd done it. This was it. She stared at the laptop, not Steve. "It's done."

Steve looked over her shoulder as she scrolled through the pages, committing the short document to memory before the information completely sank in.

"You got all that?" His brow furrowed as if he were confused. Or was it disdain that he couldn't deal with her freakish handicap?

"It doesn't seem to be important, after all. This file is a personal journal." She ignored the instinct to smooth the wrinkles or ask what he'd been thinking. "I don't know why someone from the FBI would want to encrypt a journal. It's titled *The Hera Project*."

His sudden stillness gave her a sick feeling in the pit of her stomach.

"Hera? Wasn't she a Greek goddess?" he asked.

She nodded.

"What does it say?"

"Queen Lamia, beloved of Zeus, was robbed of her child by Hera. The cunning Lamia is smarter than the jealous Hera. She will find her son… Wait. The person who encrypted this file didn't copy the myth correctly. In Greek mythology, Hera stole Lamia's *children*, not child. And Lamia disguised herself as a vampire and stole *other* children."

"Anything else?" His Adam's apple moved slowly up and down as he swallowed hard.

"It mentions the Norse myth of Fensalir," she continued. "It's the mansion of Frega where happily married couples spend—"

"Eternity together." His words escaped on an unbelieving breath. "That's the name of Stubblefield's ranch."

"She's the agent you've been in contact with. What does this journal have to do—"

"It's her. Stubblefield kidnapped your son."

"How can you be certain?"

"I'm calling George." He dialed the cell he pulled from his pocket. "E-mail that file to the Bureau."

She knew the e-mail address from searching the files earlier.

"Why would she do this?" she asked. There wasn't an answer. Steve was on the phone, explaining everything to his partner.

"How should I know?"

She could only hear Steve's side of the conversation, but she could complete the blanks. Especially when he said, "No. Have the locals pick her up here."

She wouldn't be left behind and would let Steve know as soon as he hung up the phone.

"And just why can't I go with you to Agent Stubblefield's ranch?"

"It would be safer if you stayed here and waited for the team."

"Why do men always say stupid things like that? I know they say it in books and movies to look like the caring… whatever. But you're saying it in real life. Would you say it if I were your partner? Is it expected or something? Some kind of unwritten code that you need to split from the woman you're with and somehow that's going to protect her?"

Steve opened his mouth to answer, but Jane pushed forward. She wouldn't allow him to get away with this.

"If I'm a liability then tell me so. If you think I'll slow you down, that you won't get Rory out alive, then just say it." She poked him in his chest. "Remember one thing though. In all those books and movies, the heroine usually saves the hero's butt at the last minute. I'd rather work with you instead of following after you like an idiot without a clue."

"You continually surprise me, Dr. Palmer." He tucked a wayward curl behind her ear. "But the answer is still no. Where's my hat and shirt?"

"Your hat?" She put her hands on her hips and blocked his way from the trailer. "Am I going with you or not?"

"It's been settled and I didn't have a choice." He tried to step around her.

She blocked his way again. "You are the most frustrating man. How can you just ignore me?"

"Ignore you? God, Jane. I haven't ever been able to ignore you." His hands gripped her arms, and he moved her out of his way. "Hightail it, Rhodes. Cops' ETA is six minutes."

"These guys are secure for the cops. Did you determine how they followed you?" Rhodes didn't hang around for the answer. He picked up the helmet and pushed his motorcycle down a dark path.

"That reminds me. Let me see your shoes, Janie."

She slipped them off. Steve twisted them into odd shapes until they heard a small pop.

"I can assume it's a GPS chip used for pets. Did Stubble-field bring you the clothes at headquarters?"

"Yes, but I'm not staying here," she said, frantic at the thought of being left behind.

"You're heading back to the team." He placed her shoes in her hands.

"*We* have to find Rory. Both of us, together." How could she tell him? How? "We can't wait for the FBI."

"I've called George. He's coming by chopper when the weather clears. I know you want Rory, but you need to trust me. Stay here."

There wasn't time.

"Rory is your son."

Chapter Fourteen

Of all the ways Jane had thought about informing Steve he was a father, shouting at him had been last on her list. She'd imagined his look of surprise as the words sank in, imagined him taking her gently in his arms.

Instead, he clamped his hand around her wrist and hauled her to Rhodes's ancient truck. There was nothing gentle about the way he shoved her, covered in mud, into the passenger seat. And nothing gentle about the stony planes of his face as he climbed in behind the wheel and drove—for a full hour.

Coward that she was, it took her that long to figure out what to say next.

"I'm so sorry to blurt it out like that, but I couldn't let you leave me behind."

"Did you lie just to get me to let you come?"

"No."

"So you've been lying for the past two days?" He stared at the back country road, as he had since they'd left San Antonio.

"I tried to tell you. There never seemed to be enough time."

"You've had four years."

"That isn't fair."

"Fair? If Rory really is my son, I've missed every moment of his life."

She couldn't answer. He was right. She should have told

him long ago. But she couldn't go back and correct her actions. Those four years were gone. They had to locate Rory, then they could think about the future.

"Did you know when you moved to Baltimore?" he asked.

"I found out about seven weeks later."

"And you're certain I'm the father?"

"Yes." Would he believe her if she told him she hadn't been with anyone else?

These questions were important for Steve, she understood his need to know the facts. But didn't they also need a plan to get Rory back from the kidnappers? "What are we going to do when we reach Stubblefield's ranch?"

"You just announced that I'm a father." His grip tightened on the steering wheel, squeaking the leather under his fingers. "I don't know how I'm supposed to think about anything. Part of me wants to believe you're lying, because that same part of me can't believe you lied to me for so long. But if you're finally telling me the truth, another part of me wants to hate you."

It was her turn to stare silently out the window. She'd never been good with people. She didn't know how to react in emotional situations. Logic didn't work. She couldn't draw from any book she'd ever read. Nothing prepared a person for an unexpected child. She'd had months to accept Rory's coming birth. Steve was working on his second hour.

"Before the kidnapping, you were bringing Rory to meet me. Weren't you?" he asked.

"Yes."

He barely heard her whisper over the road noise and wipers thumping against the glass. "It must have been hard all on your own."

"I had Rory." She reached up and touched his arm. "I didn't want to impose on you, Steve. I still don't."

Now how was he supposed to take that? Jane didn't

want anything from him—then or now. He could drive himself nuts.

"It didn't take more than my pregnancy to..." She let her hand drift away. "To find out what it's like to be completely alone. I wanted to be closer in case something happened to me. That's all. So Rory would have family."

Never again, he silently vowed. She'd never be alone again.

"God, Jane. You should have told me."

"I didn't know how."

"You're the smartest person I've ever met. You couldn't pick up a phone?"

"Four years ago you made it very clear that you had a job to do and that nothing would interfere."

"It's just a job."

"It never seemed as if it were 'just a job' to you," she mumbled.

But he understood. He'd tell her later how wrong he'd been. How wrong they'd both been. Nothing was more important than her and Rory.

The rain came down in earnest again. It was the first time he'd been thankful for the bad weather. Hoping it would keep planes in the area grounded. But it would also ground the Bureau's helicopters. He slowed the old truck to see through the downpour. He didn't want to miss the road that would lead them to their son.

He had a son and now he had to concentrate on his rescue.

Jane fiddled with the window handle. She hadn't really met his eyes since she'd told him about Rory. She kept blaming herself for the kidnapping, but it wasn't her...

"I'm not certain how Agent Stubblefield found out about Rory."

"*I* told Stubblefield about you." He hit the steering wheel with the palm of his hand. "I can't believe she hates me that much. I've been so stupid."

He had been stupid, running around like a chicken with his head cut off. Cliché, but true. If he'd had any brains left, he would have paid attention to the signs that Stubblefield was freaking out. He was a better agent than what he'd shown Jane the past couple of days.

"Agent Stubblefield's elaborate planning suggests it's a bit deeper than simple hatred," Jane said in a detached, doctor-like voice. "Would you mind telling me about your relationship with her? Don't partners get close?"

"Not me." Her bland tone didn't infer if she cared if he'd been involved or not. His, however, was much too defensive for a man with nothing to hide. But she didn't even raise an eyebrow.

Jane was slipping further behind her detached façade with each word. Couldn't she be the scientist *and* a woman? But she was used to handling situations on her own, not depending on anyone. And his sending her to Baltimore had played right into the scenario.

"Nothing happened. I lived in the same house with Stubblefield for two months undercover and nothing happened. When she wanted to make more of it, I told her I was in— That I was involved with you."

He'd almost told Jane he'd been in love with her. *And why don't you spill it? When do you intend on letting her in on that big secret?*

His entire life passed before Steve in the blink of an eye. Somehow he'd seen a glimpse of what he knew he wanted. A life with Jane and Rory. Maybe someday a little girl with Jane's naturally curly hair. Or a couple more boys. Memories of Jane pregnant with his child would be nice, but it didn't matter to him if Rory was the only one. He ached to show her how much he loved her.

Stubblefield wasn't going to rob him of any more of his life. The world suddenly quit spinning out of control. He knew what he had to do.

"What happened then?" she asked, interrupting his thoughts.

"The assignment ended. No big deal. No threats. Then she requested another partner. Just work." *Hadn't it been?* He didn't know anymore. "I never mentioned why she wanted the transfer. I never knew anything was wrong."

"I don't think she planned this to take revenge, Steve. I'm taking a wild leap here, but she's stolen your child. She went to elaborate means to establish that I'm crazy, on antipsychotic medication, that I'm involved in a kidnapping and murder."

She paused long enough for the wipers to swipe twice. Long enough for him to assume she was compiling facts, not merely theorizing.

"She wants *you* alive and me dead. There have been several case studies that would suggest she's done all this *for* you."

"Me? But we've never—"

"That wouldn't matter. She might be attempting to create the perfect world in which you would love her." She rubbed the bridge of her nose as if searching for glasses to push back into place. "Perhaps she used her FBI resources and discovered I had Rory. That might be what triggered a psychotic break."

More uncomfortable by the minute, he studied each sign trying to remember the exact route he and George had followed. He'd never imagined that he would become a part of the sickness growing worse in humanity. That because of him, his son would be kidnapped. Yet here he was, in the midst of a parent's worst nightmare.

"Are you certain Agent Stubblefield inherited the ranch?" she asked.

"She said she did. Last year, from an uncle."

"I don't think it's mere coincidence that you were raised on a ranch and she inherited one."

"There's no way she could afford to buy a ranch this size on what she makes at the Bureau," he confirmed. "Not unless she stole before."

"This is only a theory, Steve. Agent Stubblefield may have

a personality disorder. She may have gotten the money another way."

"She only received the Brant money two days ago. Do you think she kidnapped for the money to buy the ranch?" Was it possible? "That would mean that somewhere along the way, a kid was snatched from his parents because of me."

"Her illness has nothing to do with you. It could have been focused on anyone. You still help your parents with their ranch, right?" She didn't wait for him to answer. "Did Agent Stubblefield want you to visit?"

"Yeah, I came out with George right after she got the place." He drummed his fingers nervously on the steering wheel. "I, um, I helped her hire a foreman."

"And you help with administrative advice. Did she ever ask what you'd do for improvements?"

"Well, yeah, I might have suggested a thing or two. Like adding a small airstrip." A knot formed in his throat. It was hard to swallow and getting worse with everything Jane confirmed. "She added one last spring."

He didn't like the idea that FBI Agent Selena Stubblefield had a sick love for him. He liked it even less that he'd completely missed it. Some agent.

"If Stubblefield does have a plane, they'll be leaving as soon as the weather lets up. Fly out low, keep it under the radar…"

"You think she's leaving the country with Rory. That's why you wouldn't wait for help."

"Great, the Guadalupe River," he said with relief. Now the conversation could concentrate on Rory's rescue. "We should be getting close."

His memory was foggy, but within the next half mile he turned left on a road that would lead them to Stubblefield's ranch. They crossed the bridge over a swollen creek. There wasn't a good place to leave the truck. A steep dropoff on either side of the gravel forced him to park on the cow path.

"You wanted a plan," he said. "I think I have one, but you aren't going to like it."

"If it involves us splitting up, then no, I'm not going to like it." Her mouth was set in a stubborn line.

"Our ultimate goal is one thing. To get Rory back. Period. Whatever it takes."

"I'll do whatever it takes."

He gripped her slender hands securely in his own, wanting to protect her—yet knowing he had to let her help. "I know you're strong enough. Do you?"

A tentative, then steady nod of her head told him she believed in herself. She had been right before. It probably *would* be the heroine coming in and saving the hero's butt at the last minute.

"It's time to actually use some of that extensive government training I've received. Unfortunately, Stubblefield knows all my moves. Even the unauthorized ones."

"So how can we use that to our advantage?"

A ROCK DUG INTO STEVE's kneecap as he shifted position at the top of a hill near Stubblefield's ranch house. He smothered the curse that came with the sharp pang.

"Is there any cell reception?" he asked.

Jane pulled the cell from her windbreaker pocket. "Nothing. Your team will find the ranch. You said they'd be here as soon as the weather allowed the helicopters to take off. Right?"

"This Glock has a safety trigger. It's a bit different than the Beretta I showed you before."

Steve spoke softly, close to Jane's ear, taking in the musky smell of her in spite of the ever-present rain. He wanted to hold her, hide her and keep her safe. But it wasn't an option. The only way to get Rory back was if they worked together. They both had jobs to do. He just hoped they both came out of this thing alive.

"You can only release the safety with your trigger finger. It automatically reengages after you fire."

"That doesn't sound like much of a safety to me." Jane took the pistol and shoved it deep into her jacket pocket.

"Just be prepared to fire if you aim it at someone."

They'd barely made it across Wasp Creek. It was rising fast behind them as it sped toward the Guadalupe. They were in a grove of mesquite, the old twigs crunched under their feet with each step toward the top of the rise. The house was about a quarter of a mile away.

"It's lit up like a light bulb factory."

"I don't see anyone passing in front of the windows. Do you think they're expecting us?"

"I think—" he pulled her back where they couldn't be seen "—that Stubblefield didn't know for certain if we would find her. All the extra lighting is just to make it more difficult in case we did. That's Stubblefield's black Jeep Cherokee under the carport."

"I'll get inside."

"She's installed a lot of extra lighting around the perimeter. You could hold a night rodeo out there in the corral." His gut churned again. He had a bad feeling that he *was* expected.

"You know she's not going to believe I'm dead without proof. You could go back, get the truck and put me in the back—"

"You wouldn't do Rory any good playing dead. You need to find him and get him safely away. I'll convince Stubblefield." He looked deep into Jane's eyes, desperately wanting to know why she hadn't told him about Rory from the beginning. "Start walking as soon as I leave. I'll get her out and away from the house so you can get in. Don't forget the car keys if you come across—"

"Steve," she interrupted with a huge smile, her eyes darting back and forth to look at each of his. "Even though you didn't write them down, I've got total recall. I can remember your instructions."

"Yeah, I bet you can." He smiled back. Glad she could laugh. But this was serious. She needed to be careful or she could get killed. "Just remember your objective is to get Rory out alive. Don't think about me. Don't take any chances. Just get him away from here."

Fear. He saw it in her eyes, felt it in his gut. But his own reaction wasn't fear for himself. This felt right. They were in control. They had a plan. He had to believe it would work. Their lips seemed to come together on their own. He hadn't consciously leaned down to meet her. Had he?

Her mouth was soft and gentle and wet. She tasted like the hot canned orange drink they'd found rolling in the floorboard of the truck.

Their passion was fueled by the desperation of a goodbye kiss. One that said more than words. A kiss that said they may never see each other again.

"Jane," he squeezed in, between deep, powerful kisses. "We have to go."

"I know," she answered before securing his lips in another long, eager liplock. She slowly backed away.

"Before you go, I need to...I need to tell you—"

He stilled her lips with his fingers. "Not now. I need to tell you, too. But not now. Not like this."

It gave him hope for the future that she couldn't let him leave without saying "I love you." But he wanted more than hurried words before he ran off into danger. Although he hadn't let himself admit it, he'd known he'd loved her from the moment he'd seen her. Jane was his.

Now he was certain he hadn't lost her. And he should tell her. Right?

A tear raced down her cheek. He caught it with the tip of his finger.

"Stay out of sight and remember your objective." God, he wanted to reassure her. Swear that they'd rush in, steal Rory back and no one would get hurt. But she'd know it was a lie.

"Promise me, Janie. No matter what else happens. Think of Rory first."

"I promise."

They held hands as their eyes said goodbye. Their fingertips were the last parts of them to touch before he ran from the grove.

He sped off through the mud and brush to the main gravel road heading toward the house. He wouldn't look back or give any indication that Jane was there. Someone might be watching. Shoot, he didn't know what kind of gear Stubblefield had. She might have night-vision goggles for all he knew.

House, barn, airplane hangar, storage shed, detached garage. Too many variables. No immediate backup. George and the team were on their way, but he didn't know how long the weather would keep them grounded. He searched for his target, Selena Stubblefield. No movement.

No more time for thinking. He was in front of the two-story house. Nothing. No one came out from hiding to confront him. The rain finally stopped and the night was silent before the horses whinnied in the corral.

A PERSON IN A YELLOW rain slicker stood on the porch and joined Steve. Even from a distance, Jane could see the loathing on Steve's face. It had to be Stubblefield.

She slapped her pocket, thankful to find the solid weight of the pistol. Did Steve need her help? Should she get close enough to hear the conversation between him and their son's kidnapper?

Breathe in. Breathe out. In. Out. Taking even breaths again, she crept in the dark, just at the edge of light.

Promise me, Janie. Think of Rory first.

Jane crawled and hid behind fence posts, expecting Selena's accomplices to jump out from the gloom and grab her. No one appeared on the horizon or in the windows of the house. Selena seemed to be alone.

IT WASN'T A MIRAGE. Flesh and blood stood behind Steve as he turned to face her. His colleague. His son's kidnapper and a murderer. He took a step toward her, regaining his train of thought. Thoughts that needed to tread carefully around this psycho.

"Where's Rory?"

With the same evil smile he'd seen on too many men he'd put behind bars, she said, "Safe. For now."

The pent-up breath he'd been holding broke free from his lungs. Relief punched through his senses as he wiped the cold sweat from his forehead.

"I was beginning to think I'd have to leave without you, Steve, darling."

"It took me a while to remember how to get here." He moved his arm behind him, ready to pull his weapon.

"You are such a funny man, Steve. I think that's why I married you."

Married? She was sicker than they'd thought.

Stubblefield had flipped. She was as delusional as Jane had believed. Maybe more so. He should have let Jane explain further about that alternate world some people lived in. Stubblefield stood before him perfect and smiling, seeming to ignore everything around them while hiding the whereabouts of his son. They could have been having a conversation at the dinner table for all the reaction she demonstrated.

"You know me, always the kidder." Was that Jane's silhouette moving through the field?

"We better finish packing." Selena turned and headed in the direction of the house.

"Right." He clenched his gun handle. "We wouldn't want to get a late—"

"Bastard!" Selena spun and fired.

Chapter Fifteen

Jane heard a car backfire. No, this wasn't the city. They were in the middle of nowhere. Steve was visible under the lights near the barn. She looked up just in time to see him crumple to the ground.

Dear God. Stubblefield had shot him.

Jane clamped her hand over her mouth to keep the fury and horror from bursting out. She fell to her knees, wondering what wild hare had ever convinced her she could help Steve or Rory. She should have listened when he tried to convince her to wait for the FBI.

Is this nightmare ever going to end? Is this one woman capable of killing everyone I love?

She loved Steve. Even when logic told her she shouldn't. They were doing the best they could. *I guess this was where a leap of faith was required.* She'd loved him four years ago, had created a beautiful baby with him and she loved him now. No matter what happened, she would love Steve Woods for the rest of her life.

Standing, she took the gun from her pocket, and fought tears of anguish burning her eyes. One step, then two. She'd capture the murderer and wait for the FBI to find Fensalir Ranch. And if Selena so much as twitched, Jane would kill her.

Miracles of miracles… Steve moved. She pushed past

a prickly shrub, gun aimed at Selena. He raised his hand, signaling her to stop before placing it on his left shoulder.

Promise me, Janie. Think of Rory first.

Part of Steve's plan was to talk Selena into disclosing Rory's location. Jane ran behind the house, and stopped to catch her breath, careful not to alert anyone who might still be inside.

God help me, where could Selena have hidden a toddler?

It was the middle of the night and Rory could be anywhere.

STEVE COULD BREATHE, SEE, and still feel every hurt in his body.

There was pain in the back of his head, but that was from the fall. Not from a bullet between his eyes. Selena was a crack shot and without a doubt could have given him an extra nostril if she'd wanted.

He did have a hole in his shirt and a bit of blood from the bullet grazing his arm.

Son of a bitch, she'd shot him and he hadn't even seen the gun. He'd thought he was in control of the situation. At least his gun was still in his jeans, but he couldn't shoot Stubblefield. She was his only lead to find Rory.

"Where's Dr. Palmer?" Selena asked.

"What?" He hoped Jane had seen his signal that he was all right. He didn't dare look in her direction, not while Stubblefield was asking about her.

Without making any sudden moves, Steve pressed his shirtsleeve into the scrape to stop the bleeding. At least it was his left arm.

"Don't play dumb with me, Steve." She walked toward him, bringing the Glock almost within the reach of his leg, but not quite. "Where's Jane Palmer?"

"Dead. The men you hired killed her. Then I killed them." He sat up and his head swam. A bit of nausea and dizziness kept him planted while Stubblefield stalked like a big cat waiting for the final kill.

"Why should I believe you?" She continued to circle. "You wouldn't tell me if your whore were waiting for you."

"Where's Rory?"

"I told you he was safe."

"Why should I believe you?" he asked, stalling for time. Think. What was she after? Why had she missed?

She paused and aimed the gun straight at his chest.

"I shouldn't believe you, but I do," he said quickly. "I know you wouldn't hurt Rory. You love…ah…our son."

He made it to one knee. He didn't think he'd hurl if he stood up, but he stayed where he was. The last thing he needed was for Stubblefield to knock him back down.

"Do you think I can see him? You know I've been away for a while." God, he hoped he could guess how to play along with the fantasy. He'd never done the repentant husband thing before. "I promise I, uh, that I won't… Well, you know. Never again."

Stubblefield relaxed her arm at her side, taking her finger off the trigger. "Just remember that if you do, I won't be waiting at home for you next time. You'll never see your son again. Let's go."

He played with the idea of letting the horses out, then he saw Jane run from the house, heading for the well lit barn.

"Can we rest a minute, Selena?" He cupped his shoulder and grimaced, trying to make her think he was worse off than he was. "I'm, ah, getting a little tired."

Just as he'd hoped, Stubblefield turned toward him and missed Jane's final dash to the far side of the barn.

"You really shouldn't push yourself so hard, Steve darling. Between the Bureau and the ranch work," she said. "You're hardly ever here for Rory."

The witch acted as if she'd forgotten she'd shot him. Let her forget. It was to their advantage if Stubblefield forgot everything.

"He wouldn't know what his father looked like if it weren't for the picture by his bed."

That was why there weren't any pictures in Jane's apartment. She'd taken them all along with Rory's things to make Jane look crazy. God, they never stood a chance against Stubblefield.

Would another question concerning Rory's whereabouts bring her back to reality? Or just piss her off? He slowly worked his left arm to make sure he could still use it. The wound felt tight, so he kept moving it, kept clenching his fist. Kept getting angrier with each wave of pain.

Where is Rory! he wanted to yell.

Stubblefield stared at him. An indescribable force seemed to be fighting behind her eyes while he watched the whites of her eyes grow in size. Her hand inched its way out of the raincoat's pocket.

He wouldn't just stand there and let her shoot him again. But she would before he could cross the distance and disarm her. And this time he would get that third nostril located right between his eyes.

He made a dash to the barn. Stubblefield fired her weapon, hitting the door as he dove to the ground.

JANE HAD SEARCHED an empty house and now an empty barn. Where else could she look?

No sound. No Rory.

Shots hit the door as Steve kicked it shut behind him. Blood saturated a portion of his left arm as he searched for something to slow Stubblefield down.

"Stubblefield's as crazy as you thought. There's no door latch. We need to get that gun away from her." He spoke in a loud whisper, heaved air into his lungs, and pointed toward her left. "Hide and come out when she's got her back to you. Quick!"

Scared to death, she ducked behind the tack room door

Pieces of broken bridles and lead ropes hung above her head. The smell of leather was strong in the small area. Without a handle, she was unable to close the door completely, allowing her to see part of the main room.

"Steve!" Stubblefield's voice called wildly.

Even muted through the wood, Jane could tell the woman was on the edge of losing it.

"I thought I heard something," Steve lied. Jane had seen his eyes. He'd been worried Selena would find her. Seen the desperation and uncertainty.

Believe him, you murderer! But Stubblefield wouldn't. Jane knew she wouldn't. Selena's two personalities were at war with each other. Faltering between the fantasy where Steve and Rory were hers and reality where she knew why he was truly here.

"You heard that whore!" Stubblefield's voice grew closer and more furious. "She followed you home."

The door hinges to the tack room squealed a short rusty song.

"It was more like ah…a bobcat." Steve was close, too.

A shadow passed in front of the door, but she couldn't tell whether it was him or Stubblefield.

"I thought it might be what's scarin' the horses. Is my shotgun in the house?"

Oh, God, Steve. Don't ask her questions. Don't make her think.

Jane couldn't hide any longer. In order to find Rory, they had to subdue Stubblefield. The woman's back was to her. This was her chance. She inched the door open without making a sound.

STEVE SHOOK HIS HEAD, trying to ward off Jane. But his movement only clued the crazy woman to step aside and look directly at Jane. Predictably, she turned and pointed her weapon. Jane dropped to the floor.

Steve kicked the underside of Selena's arm with every bit of strength he had left. He forced the gun from her fingers and saw it land well out of reach near the wall.

Stubblefield screamed and leaped on top of him, knocking him backward into a sawhorse, pulling a saddle and blanket to the floor. Steve gripped one of her arms and kept it from punching him. But she twisted, turned and eventually straddled his stomach, gaining the use of both hands again.

He lost track of Jane, but hoped she still had the Glock and would stop this two-legged bobcat from tearing open his shoulder.

"Anytime now, Jane."

"Hold it!" the true mother of his son shouted. "I said, hold it!"

But it didn't slow down the woman on top of him.

"How does it feel having your child lost?" Stubblefield dug her nails into his arm, clawing skin as she ripped his shirt from his wound.

"You bastard! You adulterer! You don't deserve to ever see your son again."

A she-devil was on his chest. Demented and out of control. Stubblefield kicked, screamed, hit and punched. She formed her hands into claws and went for his eyes. In self-defense, he closed them and tried to buck her off. Her nails tore into his face. He punched blindly, not daring to actually look for a target.

"Aren't *I* the one you want to tear apart?" Jane yelled.

The unfamiliar malice in Jane's voice got his attention. It caused Stubblefield to look toward her just in time to catch a mouth full of bridle Jane swung through the air like a baseball bat.

Stubblefield fell off him with the force from Jane's blow, sprang to her feet like a cat and slowly advanced.

"You won't shoot me, bitch. You need me to find that whelp you call a son." Stubblefield sounded possessed. Something straight from a B movie. Her speech was guttural, her hair frenzied from their fight. She shrugged her shoulders out of the raincoat, letting it fall to the floor, and stalked Jane, who still held the bridle in one hand and the Glock in the other.

"Pull the trigger!" Steve shouted.

Jane froze. He saw the hesitation in her eyes and the shaking of her hands. Stubblefield crept forward, yet Jane's body didn't shift an inch.

"You've taken enough from me, Stubblefield." He stood, catching her attention, and dove for her body. They landed against the wall, tack falling on top of them.

She was stronger than he'd thought. Maybe he was just more tired. Stubblefield's formal defense training seemed to have disappeared as they rolled in the dirt. She fought like a demented stranger, someone he'd never seen before. Several of her blows landed against his left shoulder and made him suck air through his teeth.

Now *he* was on top and there was no way she could throw him off. His forearm went under her chin, cutting off her air.

"Where's Rory?" he asked through gritted teeth.

But she shook her head and squeaked out, "Never."

Everything changed.

Eyes wide, she stared at him with a look of wonder as if she couldn't believe he would kill her. He could see her thoughts. Then the realization that he just might choke her to death sank in. She clawed furiously at his arm, but couldn't budge him. Her struggles grew weaker.

He kept his arm in place. Agent Selena Stubblefield was asphyxiating—and for an instant he wanted her to.

Arms falling to her sides, eyes closed, she looked peaceful lying in the dirt—sane and unable to hurt anyone else. He backed off and saw the involuntary drawing of breath. Jane immediately knelt beside them and felt for a pulse.

"She's just unconscious." He stood, wobbled and leaned against the wall. Then he scrubbed his face and pushed his hair back. "We need to tie her up."

Steve leaned heavily on the wall and made his way back to the tack room for rope. His body felt like roadkill. His left arm in particular hung at his side like a dead armadillo.

"I thought I could do it. But she was right." Jane joined him and put her arms around his waist, burying her face in what was left of his shirt. "I wanted to kill her for everything she's done. But I just couldn't pull the trigger."

"There's nothing wrong with that, Janie. We'll find Rory." He grabbed some tack to tie up Stubblefield. "If it takes the entire FBI combing this place inch by inch, we'll find him."

He heard the barn door swing open and turned to catch Stubblefield's backside as she hauled ass toward the hangar.

"Why did I leave her alone?" He ran to the open outside door. Stubblefield was running like a wild Mustang and he was already breathing hard. He'd never catch her. "Call George from the house."

"The line's dead," Jane shouted, and dangled something in her hand. She had the keys to the Cherokee parked at the house.

They ran as fast as they could to the detached garage. Just as they slammed the Jeep doors, he heard an engine rev and wheels squeal over concrete. But where was Rory?

Stubblefield wouldn't have left him. She'd been scratching Steve's eyes out to keep him from ever seeing his son again. He could see the top of a car seat through the back window of the Camry. She had Rory with her. Stubblefield made it to the main drive and floored the gas. She soared over the small rise by the mesquite grove.

They topped the hill in time to see Stubblefield's brake lights as she swerved away from Rhodes's truck that blocked the driveway. Steve couldn't speak. He watched the unbelievable scene played out in front of him. The car fishtailed in the mud and continued sliding. There was nothing to stop it from plunging straight into the swollen creek. It sank into the raging water, and was quickly swept downstream.

Leaping from the Jeep, he reached the bank at the same time Jane did. He skidded to a stop and yanked at his boots.

"You aren't going after her?" Jane told him more than asked.

She hadn't seen.

"There was a car seat."

Chapter Sixteen

"God, no." Jane tugged off her shoes and jacket, prepared to rescue their son. This was her fault. If she hadn't insisted on helping Steve… If they'd waited… "Oh, my God, he'll die."

Steve turned her to face him. He squeezed her arms, his face tortured with fear and longing.

"We're not certain he's in the car. I'm begging you to stay here." He released her, stepping to the edge of the creek. For an instant he paused, his gaze finding and holding hers. "I love you."

The swirling water sent him spiraling downstream and jerked him under. The map she'd committed to memory indicated that Wasp Creek had intermittent water. It didn't list depth, but it didn't take a genius to know that it was prone to flash flooding.

There was no sign of the car. It had to be completely submerged. She couldn't see anything. Headlights. She ran back to the Jeep and drove it as close to the creek as she dared.

How long could Steve hold his breath?

Jane followed him into the water and was swiftly pulled under. She tried to find the car, Steve, Rory. Her weak stroke was no match for the current which swept her from the bank. She couldn't see anything and latched on to a log, pulling herself to shore.

Her knees gave way and she collapsed in a heap next to

a tree. If she began crying, she wouldn't be able to stop. She concentrated on taking one breath after another.

The tree next to her was rough against her skin. Insects began to call to one another, and the sound of the raging current filled a night that was finally clear.

A typical night, but nothing was normal.

"Please, God. Please, God." She couldn't think of any other words to say. Where was Steve?

If her son died in that creek, it would be her fault.

GRIEF BROADSIDED HIM like an eighteen-wheeler. He hoped Stubblefield burned in hell for killing his son. He had minimal vision in the dark murky water as he smashed into the side of the busted hood. He could see in a dim, distorted fashion the car was jammed at an angle—front end lower—into a narrow portion of the creek.

Suddenly the headlights reflected off the mud. The interior lights flashed on, then off, then on. The water must be shorting out the electrical system. He worked his way around to the driver's side and pulled at the door handles.

The door was wedged shut or locked. Either way, it wasn't budging.

Selena was still behind the wheel struggling to free herself. Water was already at her chin. He banged on the window, pointing at the door.

"Help me!" she screamed, her eyes desperate when she looked at him. She pulled at the seat belt, but never pushed buttons for the door locks or windows. "I don't want to die! Help me!"

The water was quickly filling the car. Rory was a bit higher and still crying in his car seat. Steve yanked at the tree limbs near the door. The car shuddered, then shifted. He didn't want the car swept farther downstream so he stopped.

Out of air, he surfaced. He pulled the switchblade from his

pocket and opened it. He took several short breaths then one deep lungful of air before diving back to the car.

Blindly he pried at the rubber seal trying to pop the glass aside.

Precious air from his lungs bubbled to the surface when he looked upon his son's face for the first time. The car was full of water and his cry had been silenced. His short brown hair flowed back and forth in slow motion. His chubby little arms seemed to wave at Steve and his eyes were closed as if in sleep.

With each beat of Steve's heart he pounded the handle between the passenger window and car frame. He needed air, but he wasn't going back up without his son.

Fighting the surging water, he dug his toes between the tree limbs on the driver's side, anchoring himself at the rear window of the flooded car.

Summoning the last vestiges of his strength, he turned upside down and used his knee to push against the glass and felt it give way. It floated into the car.

Air.

He needed air.

So did his son.

THEY WERE DEAD.

All of them.

There was no way Steve could hold his breath for that long. She thought he'd surfaced about thirty feet downstream and had run in that direction. But now there wasn't anything.

No sign of a car. No Steve. No bodies.

Jane paced the creek bank, rocks stabbing her bare feet. She dodged the low limbs, hanging on to them when she had to step into the water.

She tried to preserve a slim thread of hope they would survive. He'd said that he loved her.

Why now and not before? He thought he wasn't going to make it. She'd jump in again, but what if he needed her?

Oh, God.

STEVE REACHED THROUGH the window. It was a tight fit, but the only way to his son. In the front, Selena's body was covered from the rushing water. She swayed with each movement of the car.

Rory's arms floated to either side of his seat as Steve cut the straps that imprisoned his son. Lungs bursting, he refused to give in to the urge to breathe. With a fist full of his son's overalls, Steve pulled Rory through the window, tucked him tight into the crook of his arm, pushed off the car and felt the vehicle being carried farther downstream.

He struggled to the surface.

"Steve!"

He barely had the strength to fill his lungs with oxygen as he struggled to keep Rory's face as much above the water as he could. Suddenly, Jane was with him in the middle of the creek. She pulled him by his belt loop. He kicked. It seemed like hours before they made it back to shore.

He choked back the mournful howl attempting to break out of his throat. Regret for a child he'd never know tore at his insides wanting to escape.

CPR. THE MEDICAL TEXT came off the shelf, opened to page 253, and stayed as a picture in Jane's mind. The pages for mouth-to-mouth resuscitation and drowning lay open next to it. CPR for a child was different from that of an adult.

She tugged Steve onto the rocky bank, leaving his legs in the water, but far enough away from the edge so he wouldn't be pulled back into the stream. He took air deep into his lungs with each breath.

"You can let go now, Steve." She pried his fingers from their son's overalls. "He's safe."

Even in the faint light, Rory's face was pale, his lips an oxygen-deprived blue. With her son in her arms, she continued up the bank and laid his head on a tuft of grass. Right behind her, Steve scrambled up the incline on his knees.

Look. Listen. Feel.

She turned Rory on his stomach and pushed upward on his back, expelling some water, then turned him on his back again. She stared at Rory's precious little face, his rosy color faded to ash. His laughing breath now completely still.

Fighting back a wave of helplessness and despair, she checked her son's carotid artery in his neck. No pulse. Steve searched her face. Could he see her doubt reflected in her eyes? She took a calming breath because *his* eyes showed too much. She could see his faith in her. But neither of them spoke. Neither of them vocalized the slim chance of reviving their son.

Two rescue breaths.

Rory's sweet rosebud lips were still blue.

Begin cardiac compressions.

She placed the heel of her hand over the lower half of his sternum and depressed his chest rapidly at a rate of one hundred times per minute. "One, two, three, four, five."

One breath every five compressions.

She pinched his nostrils closed, covered his mouth with hers and blew.

"Breathe," Steve said like a prayer.

"Steve, I need you to breathe for him." Jane found Rory's sternum again, repositioned her hand. "One, two, three…"

Steve was in place, but looking lost. "It's been a while since… Never on a kid."

"…four, five. Come on, Rory." She demonstrated a breath for him. "Don't be afraid to blow, but not too hard and don't tilt his neck back any farther. He's in the correct position."

"One, two, three, four, five."

Tears mixed with the creek water dripping from her hair. She couldn't see. She kept her hand in place on Rory's chest and wiped at her eyes with the other while Steve blew oxygen into their son's lungs.

She didn't care how long it took. She wouldn't stop.

"Breathe, Rory," she said as much to convince herself as Steve. His strong hand shook on Rory's chin.

"Kids are resilient. He can do this."

She watched Steve blow a steady breath into Rory's mouth. She felt his little body jerk. She checked his pulse. "It's weak, but there. Keep breathing for him."

Steve blew three more breaths.

Rory coughed. He was back. Jane rolled him to his tiny side and he coughed water from his lungs.

"Thank God," Steve sighed in front of her.

Rory whimpered. Cried. Threw up. Screamed. It was the most heavenly sound in the world.

Lifting Rory to her lap, she turned him facedown and patted his back as he continued to cry between coughs to get up more fluid. Rory cried and fussed to be lifted. "Just a bit more, sweetheart. You need to get all that nasty water out." She wondered if he actually understood the danger he'd been in.

Then it hit her. Not just danger. He'd died. Her precious little boy had died. She tried not to hurt him when she hugged him close to her chest and remembered how good it was to have him in her arms.

Steve kissed her forehead, then feebly stood.

Jane clung tight to their little boy. Steve wouldn't risk his life to save the woman who wanted her dead? Was he really considering it? She grabbed his arm, intent on not letting him out of her sight.

Mixed emotions coursed through her. Agent Stubblefield had stolen her son. But Jane wanted to preserve life, not… Selena had tried to kill them and had succeeded in murdering others. "Is there any chance for her?"

"The car was swept downstream. I barely got Rory out. Another thirty seconds…" They slowly walked up the bank.

"I don't want to lose you, Steve."

"You won't."

"I love you." She had to tell him. Had to say the words aloud and should have told him earlier. She should have said them four years ago.

She didn't need a response from him. He had so much to process. *I'm not here for me. As long as he accepts Rory, that's all that matters.*

"What do we do now?" she asked.

"Wait at the house. Hear any bugles? Or choppers? This is one time I wish the cavalry would ride up over the hill."

"How long?" She tried to calm Rory, but she couldn't even calm herself. "He's normally not this fussy."

"It's a beautiful noise."

She couldn't tell what his reaction was to Rory. Too much had happened. Steve looked around on the ground, most likely searching for his boots.

"Here, you take Rory back to the car. You both need to warm up." Jane caught up with Steve and handed him their son. "I'll find our shoes."

Steve walked back to the vehicle. "Everything's okay now Rory." Holding kids wasn't a new thing for him. Between his family and his job, he'd held hundreds of children, but this was different. How did he begin to catch up?

He snagged Jane's jacket along the way. He removed the 9 mm and stuffed it in his jeans at the small of his back, then climbed into the Jeep. He turned the key and cranked the heat. He peeled the cutesy clothes off that no kid should be forced to wear. Then he wrapped his son in the windbreaker Rhodes had loaned Jane.

The kid was a squirmer. He didn't want to lie peacefully in Steve's arms. It had to be a good sign that he fought to climb all over him and the steering wheel.

God Almighty, what would it be like to be a father? He hadn't allowed himself to think of that possibility. And now... Shoot, he was too tired to think about it.

But he'd gladly take it on with Jane's help. She'd said she loved him. That was a start, right?

"Hey, kid." He pushed his hair back from his face as Rory looked up at him. "Meet your dad."

Rory's small hand scrapped the stubble on his cheek and skimmed his nose. "Mommy says you're my daddy."

Something smacked his heart and twisted it in his chest. This feeling was totally different than anything he'd ever felt before. Indescribable? You bet. Impossible for words.

But it felt good. As if a piece of him had been missing and he hadn't known it. Then suddenly his puzzle was complete and wham! He was sunk and would never be the same again.

"That's you, kid. You're one of my missing pieces. And your mom's the other." He gently mussed Rory's damp hair.

"There's still no cell coverage," Jane said as she got into the Jeep.

"Let's go to the house and I'll see if I can reconnect the phone." He cupped her cheek and she rested her head there for a moment.

She hugged Rory and placed several kisses on his face. "You don't suppose she has a Jet Ski handy to ford that creek, do you?"

"In a big hurry to leave?" Steve tried to joke, but one look at Jane's face told him how serious she was.

"That house is...creepy." She hugged Rory closer. "I think I'd rather wait for you in the car."

"I'll see if I can get the phone working and verify that the team is on the way." He pulled under the carport and left the engine running to keep them warm. "You stay here while I check out the house. I want to make sure there aren't any more surprises."

"I've already been inside, Steve. No one was there."

"Let me check it out." After squishing his wet socks back into his boots, he pushed the auto-lock and shut the door before she could argue anymore. His boots would never be the same.

The door wasn't shut all the way so he pushed it open, hesitating when it hit the cabinets. He had no reason to think Selena was working with someone. He was just tired and a little spooked because Jane thought the house was creepy.

Hired guns, forged documents, murder. Selena could handle all that and more. What was it that Jane had said about schizophrenics? They were usually brilliant people while they kept their worlds separate. It was only when those worlds collided that they had problems.

He mounted the stairs and checked out the upper floor. Each room had the pictures that came with the frame, but the faces had been changed. Seeing his face in a wedding photo with Stubblefield made him gag a little. Seeing a fake birth certificate with Stubblefield's name on it had turned his stomach.

Understanding perfectly why Jane had felt creeped out, he headed back downstairs. Two more rooms, then he could check on the telephone.

The living room was straight from a home design magazine. He lifted a picture of the woman he'd trusted as a partner. More craziness. He pulled Selena's face from the glass and let it fall to the carpet. The true picture was of a beautiful smiling and very pregnant Jane.

Sick. Stubblefield was—had been—very sick.

He picked up the smaller photo of… The vase in front of him shattered, and the overhead lights went out.

"What the…?" He turned just in time to see an arm pointing a pistol at him as he dove for cover near the window. He tipped the coffee table to its side, pulled the 9 mm from his waistband and returned a couple of shots.

"I don't know what trouble you're in, man. But killing me ain't the way to get rid of it."

"Oh, but it is, Agent Woods. One should never trust a crazy woman to follow through on her word," the man sneered and popped two more rounds in Steve's direction. "First you, then Jane."

Steve threw some odd metal art object through the windowpane, but would probably get shot if he attempted to leave the room that way. "Selena's dead, man. And I don't have any beef with you."

"I surmised as much about Agent Stubblefield. And your *beef* with me, Woods, is the simple fact that you are not dead. Yet."

The next shot was closer. Steve was pinned down between the couch and table. Nowhere to go.

"Not dead?"

The man's shots were getting too close for comfort. The wood of the table wasn't going to be much of a barrier for long.

"Yes, you need to be dead. That is the general conclusion one should make when someone is shooting at you." The man's voice was cultured, eastern seaboard and condescending.

"Who are you, man?"

"You want me to disclose all, Agent Woods? First tell me where you left Jane and Rory."

Where had he left... So the guy hadn't seen them drive up. At least they were okay.

"Naw, this is a one-for-one exchange, man. You know who I am. It's only fair you tell me who you are." Steve fired two rounds, shattering a picture on the wall behind the shooter's position. Then he pulled the table closer to the couch and barricaded himself a bit more.

"I'm surprised you haven't already taken a wild guess," the gunman said safely from the hallway.

"Okay, if you won't admit who you are, you could at least tell me why you want us dead."

The guy pumped six or seven rounds at the table—the last two ripped through and hit Steve's previous position. This guy knew what he was doing with a gun and had him pinned. He checked his clip.

Four more.

Steve waited for him to fire again, leaping over the table a split second after the last shot hit the wall behind him. He fired twice while running. Four-letter words shouted through his brain as he rolled through the doorway on his left shoulder. But he'd made it across the hallway to the kitchen without being hit by the man's rapid fire.

"I'm afraid it's time to end this game, Agent Woods," the man called from the hall as Steve ran for the back door.

No harm in retreating.

Sure enough, the Jeep was empty of both Jane and keys. Steve zigzagged as fast as he could while firing the last of his ammo at his unknown assassin. He headed straight to the barn where Stubblefield's weapon had fallen.

He pulled the door open and faced a gun barrel.

"My God, Steve." Jane lowered the pistol and backed into the barn. "I saw you turn lights on upstairs, then a shadow passed the kitchen window. When the shooting began, I ran out here for the gun." She reached for his wound, but he didn't have time to think about it. "Are you all right? Your shoulder's bleeding again."

Jane released the Glock into Steve's grip. He immediately went to the door and looked toward the house. No one in sight.

"Is Rory safe?" he asked in an exhausted whisper and she nodded. "Did you get a look at this guy?"

"No, she didn't, Agent Woods."

The man chasing him had used the corral entrance to the barn. In his mid-forties, his medium build still looked in excellent physical condition. In Steve's present shape, he'd have a difficult time going head to head with him.

"Hayden?" Jane turned and couldn't believe her eyes. This was her friend holding a gun on them. "What are you doing?"

"Realizing a dream, my dear." He motioned at Steve, who promptly dropped his weapon and tossed it slightly to her right. "Now if you don't mind placing your hands where I can see them and telling me where Rory is? It wouldn't do for him not to be included in this little reunion."

"You want the serum," she said, disgusted. He'd called it her unrealized dream. Had encouraged her on several occasions to sell out to the highest bidder. "You worked with Selena? How?"

"You didn't really believe that woman of below average intelligence was behind a complicated plot, now did you?" Hayden said. "Dear Jane, I've already got the serum. The formula was in the hands of its new owners yesterday. And your hands, Agent Woods." He gestured with the barrel of his gun that he wanted them above Steve's head.

"Steve can't lift his arm. He's been shot," she said. He was also faking, since he'd used his arm several times. And he was extremely silent. She'd never quite seen the look currently on his face before. Hatred combined with vengeance.

"He's about to be again." Hayden laughed.

"Just one thing to satisfy my curiosity, Hughes," Steve said. "How did you hook up with Stubblefield?"

"Selena approached me several months ago after performing a background check on Jane. Her obsession was so obvious. She needed money to finance her romantic delusions. I needed her delusions to obtain the formula and Rory." He spat his words at her. "I never imagined you were so naive, Jane. Your formula is worth millions. And the possibilities with a gifted child like Rory are unending. He will be brilliant and I'll be right there to exploit every thought."

"I trusted you. You know the dangers of the serum. I even confided in you about Rory. You encouraged me to move back to Dallas to be with Steve."

"All a part of the plan after you rejected my proposal. I would have been a good father figure."

"You wanted control over Rory. I couldn't let that happen." He and Selena had been planning the kidnapping and how to frame her for months.

"It should have been easy enough to eliminate you so my control of the formula and Rory would never be questioned," Hayden clarified. "But that incompetent bitch Stubblefield was too cheap to hire true professionals who would kill you. So now it's up to me."

"In my business we call it murder, Hughes. You afraid to say it?" Steve moved between her and Hayden's gun. He kept his injured arm behind his back. He pointed first toward her and then the gun on the ground.

"How noble. Enough talk." Anger made the veins in Hayden's neck bulge. "I can't waste any more of my time. Where's Rory?" he shouted and waved the gun barrel in the air.

Steve took a running leap at Hayden and knocked him to the ground. Jane fell on the gun tossed near them. She had to protect Rory and Steve.

Hayden's gun fired.

She struggled to her feet amidst the empty buckets that had scattered and aimed her gun at Hayden.

He pulled his trigger.

So did she.

Chapter Seventeen

Jane's wrist throbbed from the recoil, and her ears rang from the blast. But she was still standing. Neither of Hayden's shots had hit her.

Opening her eyes, she saw the two men lying side by side on the hay-strewn floor. Rory cried from the next room. Hayden moaned and Steve lay motionless. *Oh, my God, did I kill him?* Or had Hayden changed the direction of his bullet and shot Steve?

Hayden reached for the gun lying near the men's heads.

"Steve!"

It was amazing Steve could move at all and his exhaustion cost him. Hayden rolled to his feet and kept Steve on the ground with a vicious kick to his ribs.

Steve was on his knees when Hayden booted him in the jaw. Jane heard the collision of heel with flesh. She watched as blood sprayed from Steve's mouth and he crashed facefirst into the dirt and hay.

Each direction Hayden turned, Jane shifted the barrel of Selena's gun to follow him. One hand steadied the other's shaking fingers that wrapped around the now-sweaty steel handle.

If she fired she might hit the wrong man, but she couldn't stand around and watch Hayden beat Steve to death. As Hayden drew his leg back for another kick aimed at Steve's stomach, she crashed into him and knocked him to the ground.

"Don't move!" She scrambled back to her feet and pointed the gun at him.

"You won't shoot me," Hayden said while he got up and staggered in her direction.

It was true. Selena had approached her the same crazy way. With that same fanatical gleam in her eyes. Jane had frozen. And then what? Selena had escaped and Rory had almost drowned.

Hayden's mouth moved, but all Jane could hear was her son's cries from behind the door. Rory wanting his mommy.

You won't shoot me, bitch! Selena's words echoed in her mind.

...do away with you, so now it's up to me. Hayden had gloated—her friend, colleague and would-be murderer.

"Don't come any closer, Hayden."

Steve appeared unconscious, slumped on the ground. She wanted him to roll over and keep Hayden away from her, but she'd hesitated too long before hitting Hayden. Steve lay unmoving and couldn't save her this time.

"We both know you won't pull that trigger."

This man wasn't her friend. The look in his eyes was deadly. He wanted one thing...to kill them.

"Don't we?"

The shot went wild—she'd closed her eyes again. But it stopped his advance. Almost too late she realized Hayden had retreated, searching for the other gun and was in close proximity to where it had fallen.

"Shoot!" Steve yelled.

She didn't take her eyes off Hayden slithering toward the gun like a snake. There was no time. She squeezed the trigger.

Hayden spun and crumpled. The scent of gunpowder was strong and strange mixed with the smell of horses and leather. Hayden's body fell near Steve's feet. He lay with his head toward her, his eyes open wide and blood seeping from a hole in his chest.

"Oh, God. I killed him." Jane let the gun fall from her numb fingers.

"You missed, sweetheart." Steve tiredly let his head drop to the ground again. "I'm really going to have to teach you how to shoot."

Hayden's gun rested on Steve's stomach. She hadn't heard him make the last shot. But he'd come to her rescue yet again.

"Go take care of Rory, hon."

Jane carefully stepped over Hayden's body and went to the tack room, scooping her son into her arms. "Oh, God, Rory. I'm so sorry. It's okay, baby."

Steve sat against the wall. She held Rory close, assuring herself he was fine. That everything was fine. At least for them. She glanced toward Hayden. She had no regrets he was dead.

"No pulse. Leave him. Crime scene," Steve commanded in short sentences using a stronger voice than his appearance credited.

His shirt was in rags. No longer white and light blue or snapped together. It was a dingy brown with bloodstains and mud streaks—just like his chest. He had a gash on his forearm, held together by duct tape. The gunshot graze was bleeding again.

Swelling and bruising on the right side of his face where Hayden had kicked him emphasized the fresh blood coming from a laceration on his lip. His hair hung limp and was tangled with straw. Scratches outlined his eyes where Selena had used her nails.

Yet, somehow he looked perfect. She'd never been happier to stare at anyone in her life.

"You're a mess," she said. "Are you all right?"

"Nothing's wrong that a week in bed won't cure. Especially with the right woman lying next to me." His lopsided smile as he winked at her, captured her heart. "Is Rory okay?"

She nodded, but continued to keep their son's eyes averted from Hayden's body. "Can we get out of here?"

"Yeah. Once I can walk." He grabbed his ribs and inched his way up the wall.

"Are you sure you can make it? Maybe I should get the Jeep and drive you back to the house?" She switched Rory to her right hip and scooted under Steve's shoulder to give him support.

"I can make it." Despite his words, Steve kept Jane under his shoulder. It felt right. Even when his hand brushed his son's warm arm. He mussed Rory's hair and dared eye contact. "Hey, kiddo."

His son looked up at him with round, trusting eyes, making him feel ten feet tall. Yeah, a giant of hurt. Shoot, there was no way he'd wimp out now. He could collapse in a chair at the house. Think about lying down at a hospital. And that week of bed rest with Jane and Rory at his side wasn't such a bad idea.

Jane's glance lingered a bit too long on Hayden's body. "He's not worth your pity," Steve said. He limped from the barn so she wouldn't stay, and hoped she wouldn't think about the betrayal of a man she trusted.

"Why would someone go to such lengths? Selena, yes. I can understand that she was driven by an unfortunate disease."

"*Unfortunate?* The psycho kidnapped and drowned your son. She murdered at least one person we know of and you believe it's understandable because of her 'unfortunate disease'? What does it take to get you angry?"

She dropped her shoulder supporting him and he nearly fell. No way. He'd said that out loud and not even realized it.

"Just because I remain calm and don't freak out at anything that goes wrong, it doesn't mean I don't *have* emotions." She took more of his weight again and continued to move toward the house. So she controlled herself and wasn't prone to temper tantrums. He could live with that.

"Hayden I can't understand," she continued. "Respect,

prestige, wealth—he had everything." She shook her head, clearly unable to accept her friend's betrayal. "The formula was only in the beginning stages. There are several like it. I'm at a complete loss who would pay millions for it."

"We'll know for certain if he had everything he claimed. Greed does unusual things to people. Something pushed Hayden over the top. If he had all the money he needed like you think, he must have been jealous." They'd never know for certain what it had been, but Steve had seen the greed and lust in the man's eyes.

He was too doggone tired to think about it any longer and they still had to wait on the Bureau. That was going to be fun. He'd be lucky if he got suspended without McCaffrey pressing charges. And he couldn't forget about the missing money either. Someone would take the blame for everything that had gone wrong, and he seemed the most likely candidate.

They were nearly at the house, nearly at a point where they'd have to seriously discuss those "I love yous" stated in the heat of the moment. He hadn't wanted to tell her like that.

How could he possibly talk to Jane about sharing his un-certain life? The intensity of the past four days might sway her decision. She might feel obligated to stay with him for a while, but he wanted more.

Could they trust each other with forever?

Dawn finally crept over the trees behind them as they reached the back door. The whirling of chopper blades bounced off the sides of the house and barn.

"Great, the cavalry's finally here," he said, wincing when he reached for the screen door. All the pain of the evening had caught up with him.

"Do you think they'll have a medic with them?" she asked, looking at his shoulder. "Is it all right to wait inside?"

"I'm okay." Although one look told him he was bleeding like a son-of-a-bitch again. "We've already been there. I think they'll give us some latitude."

Jane looked calm enough as she pulled out a chair, set Rory in his lap, and found a kitchen towel. But her hands shook as she pressed it against his wound.

He did feel a bit light-headed.

No two ways about it. He was walking on cut glass. She wanted to talk, he could tell. Her eyes questioned him each time they met his as she sat Rory nearby in a chair.

He just couldn't make his mouth work.

For some reason he was scared to death to have an uninterrupted conversation with Jane about their past or future. Facing another perp—even while he felt as if he'd been at the bottom of a stampede—was preferable to being turned down by her.

"There's no telling how long it'll be before we get a real chance to talk." He stretched out his right hand to pull her to his lap. The towel fell to the table. She lifted it and put pressure on his shoulder again.

"What's wrong with now?" she asked, concentrating on his shoulder.

"I might pass out and miss something important." It wasn't a joke, even though she harrumphed as if it were. "I want to take Rory to meet my parents."

His hand around her waist felt a catch in her breath. God, he was just too tired to figure out what was wrong this time.

"Of course. Sure. It'll give me time—"

"Hey. I didn't mean alone." In spite of the urge to lean his head on her shoulder and fall asleep, he drew her close and kissed her. "You're not going to leave me to watch a three-year-old all by myself, are you? I'd never survive."

"You would survive anything."

"You're wrong," he said as he guided her face closer to kiss her again. "Without you, I didn't—"

"So we do have survivors," McCaffrey said as he holstered his 9 mm and joined them. "I'm assuming that since you're both sitting here, that the rest of the house is clear?"

Steve nodded and Jane stood. He should give a report. There was something important he needed to say…

"Thanks for the file. George is tracking down the illegal sale of your new drug, Dr. Palmer. It seems Hayden Hughes…"

McCaffrey's voice dropped into oblivion. Black spots swam in front of Steve's eyes as he slid from the chair, landing on his butt and whacking the back of his noggin.

"We need a med-evac ASAP."

"There's somethin' I need to say…" He couldn't remember.

He was just too tired.

Chapter Eighteen

Jane strolled under the trees on the ranch where Steve had grown up. He'd played here. Learned to be a man here. He'd climbed one of these giants as a kid, fallen and broken his arm. He had roots as deep as the line of oaks that had been planted a hundred years ago.

"I don't belong here." The words tumbled out on a deep breath meant to hold the tears inside.

She'd learned a lot about Steve from his family. They'd all come this weekend to meet Rory. His parents, siblings, nieces and nephew, every cousin, aunt, uncle and grandpa. On one hand it was nice to be accepted and treated like more than the mother of Steve's child.

On the other, it was a bit overwhelming for someone who was raised with no family other than her parents. No home to go back to because they'd moved from state to state to be closer to the best schools. She didn't know how to act around all the shared Woods familiarity.

They were warm, loving and accepting and she was totally out of her league.

She ached for the sense of belonging this family freely offered. They had opened their home and hearts. And her heart belonged to the man crossing the yard to join her. Dressed in his working boots, worn jeans, an old FBI T-shirt and that ever-present Stetson. Steve Woods had forever captured her heart.

"How 'bout that sunset," Steve said.

"I thought you were playing with Rory." Small talk seemed to be all they'd managed this past week.

Just as Steve had predicted, between the hospital, debriefing by the FBI and meeting family, there hadn't been much private time for them.

"Mom wanted some more time with him." He pointed near the house where Amanda pushed Rory in the rope swing. Steve's honest smile made her heart beat faster.

The scratches were healed, the bruises fading to yellow on Steve's handsome face. He'd nearly died. He'd risked everything for her and Rory, more than once. She wanted so much to run into his arms and never leave.

She loved him.

"McCaffrey called." He stuck his hands in his jeans pockets as he had so often when around her. "Thomas Brant is back with his family along with their money. It was found in a briefcase in Selena's car. Hughes had contact with her as early as ten months ago. They've exonerated you of all charges. And I'm cleared to go back to work."

Everything was wrapped up. She could return to her apartment and begin work. Her eyes watered while she viewed the sunset he admired. Definitely beautiful, reflecting every color imaginable off the clouds.

"I thought you'd be happy." He caught her hand, swinging her around to face him, but quickly let go.

"I'm happy." She knew her voice didn't convey a happy tone. It was shaky, holding back the tears that still threatened her control.

He shrugged his shoulders and cocked an eyebrow as if he didn't believe her.

"We haven't really gotten to talk yet." He wrenched his hat from his head and began his customary pacing. Crushing acorn shells and crunching his hat brim with every footstep. "You know, fours years ago, I never thought I'd get the chance to see you again. Then you were back in my life and trying to save your…trying to save Rory."

The same feeling of inadequacy slammed her, shutting down her brain, keeping her mouth from forming words.

"You should have told me," Steve said softly.

"You're right." It was time to tell him everything. "I thought I could raise Rory myself. Protect him like my parents protected me."

"You didn't think I could do that?" He set his hat on a fence post.

She looked toward the house, her eyes drawn to the swing and her son. She heard the crunching of shells behind her. "Oh, no, Steve. It wasn't anything like that. It was the only way I knew to survive. The habit of moving on and not looking back. I've never had a place to look back to."

"What made you change your mind?"

"Hayden had Rory's IQ tested without my consent. When the tests concluded Rory was like me, I understood why my parents were so protective and kept my gift a secret. We were never romantically involved. Suddenly Hayden wanted to become a family to be there for Rory. I realized my son already had a family. He needed his father."

Without skipping a beat, Steve stepped in front of her and stared at her mouth. His brown eyes caused a hitch in her breathing, just before his lips captured hers. Her hunger for him was all-embracing. She wanted every morsel of his mouth, his hands, his body. She didn't want the kiss to end, but Steve leaned back with that dazzling smile splashed on his face.

He stuck his hand in his front pocket again and pulled out a diamond ring. "So, are you going to marry me?"

I want to. I didn't think it would matter, but it does. She craved to, but it was a hard question to answer. She'd thought about it since she first considered moving back to Dallas.

"I can't. As much as I want to, I came back to change Rory's life. I never meant to change yours."

"Maybe my life could use a little changing." He stepped back, one hand pushing through his hair, the other tucking the ring in his jeans. "Maybe it's the concussion, but I'm not completely following you."

"I don't want to get married because you feel obligated by the fact we had a child together." She wanted to comfort him, to kiss him again, to hold on to him forever. But she didn't. She stayed where she was and said the words she'd practiced in her head too many times to count. "Go back to saving the world one case at a time, Steve. Rory will visit any time you want."

"And what about what *I* want?"

"How could you possibly know what you want?" The words seemed familiar. It took a split second, but she remembered where she'd heard those words before. Steve had said them four years ago when they'd spoken about her career.

"I want what's best for you and Rory." He shook his head and let out a long breath. "I made the decision that broke us up. Let's make this one to stay together."

"You hardly know us," she whispered.

"That can change." He slapped his hand against his thigh. "Why are you so dead set against us being together?"

"It's not that. You're an FBI agent who has a gift for finding children and reuniting them with their families. I don't want to change you or stop you from what you love. You'd eventually resent me for taking you away from your work."

He cupped her face in his hands, waiting until her eyes met his.

"Look at me. Analyze the muscles in my face to determine if I'm telling the truth." Steve took a deep breath and exhaled slowly before he said the most important words in his life. "I love you. And I loved Rory before I knew he was my son. I loved him because he was *your* son."

"But you didn't say anything when I told you."

"It was kind of a shock to my brain. I'll admit it took me a while to focus. And I didn't completely understand until now why you didn't tell me."

Tears finally escaped the confines of her beautiful eyes. He knew how she felt. He remembered when Rory first spoke to him. How real everything became when he held the little guy in his arms for the first time.

"But you can't just ask me to marry you."

His mom waved from across the yard and pointed to his son running toward them. They all deserved the chance to be a family. "Why not? You love me, don't you?"

"Yes, but—" She turned away, but he caught the look of fear and hope on her face. Caught the way her arms hugged her middle, protecting herself.

"No buts. Just say yes." He caught her shoulders and tucked her safely against his chest, whispering in her ear. "When are you going to stop running, Janie?"

"I'm not running anywhere." She turned in his arms, searching his face.

"You're running from me and I can't let you go again."

He fingered the ring in his pocket, bringing it out one last time. His hand found hers, poised between them…ready to accept his promise.

"I don't know how to do this," she said with a shaky voice.

Sliding the ring onto her finger was the commitment he wanted to give. It was the right choice for him. Her acceptance by wearing the ring was what he needed.

Jane smiled as she sealed their pledge. They'd discover— together—how to make it right for them both.

"Let's start with a kiss and take a slow walk down the aisle."

* * * * *

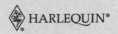 HARLEQUIN®

INTRIGUE®

COMING NEXT MONTH

Available October 12, 2010

#1233 CHRISTMAS COUNTDOWN
Bodyguard of the Month
Jan Hambright

#1234 BOOTS AND BULLETS
Whitehorse, Montana: Winchester Ranch Reloaded
B.J. Daniels

#1235 THE SPY WHO SAVED CHRISTMAS
Dana Marton

#1236 SILENT NIGHT STAKEOUT
Kerry Connor

#1237 DOUBLE-EDGED DETECTIVE
The Delancey Dynasty
Mallory Kane

#1238 A COP IN HER STOCKING
Ann Voss Peterson

LARGER-PRINT BOOKS!

GET 2 FREE LARGER-PRINT NOVELS

PLUS 2 FREE GIFTS!

Breathtaking Romantic Suspense

HARLEQUIN®

A Romance

FOR EVERY MOOD™

Spotlight on

Inspirational

Wholesome romances
that touch the heart and soul.

See the next page
to enjoy a sneak peek from
the Love Inspired® inspirational series.

*See below for a sneak peek at
our inspirational line, Love Inspired®.
Introducing HIS HOLIDAY BRIDE
by bestselling author Jillian Hart*

Autumn Granger gave her horse rein to slide toward the town's new sheriff.

"Hey, there." The man in a brand-new Stetson, black T-shirt, jeans and riding boots held up a hand in greeting. He stepped away from his four-wheel drive with "Sheriff" in black on the doors and waded through the grasses. "I'm new around here."

"I'm Autumn Granger."

"Nice to meet you, Miss Granger. I'm Ford Sherman, from Chicago." He knuckled back his hat, revealing the most handsome face she'd ever seen. Big blue eyes contrasted with his sun-tanned complexion.

"I'm guessing you haven't seen much open land. Out here, you've got to keep an eye on cows or they're going to tear your vehicle apart."

"What?" He whipped around. Sure enough, mammoth black-and-white creatures had started to gnaw on his four-wheel drive. They clustered like a mob, mouths and tongues and teeth bent on destruction. One cow tried to pry the wiper off the windshield, another chewed on the side mirror. Several leaned through the open window, licking the seats.

"Move along, little dogie." He didn't know the first thing about cattle.

The entire herd swiveled their heads to study him curiously. Not a single hoof shifted. The animals soon returned to chewing, licking, digging through his possessions.

Autumn laughed, a warm and wonderful sound. "Thanks,

I needed that." She then pulled a bag from behind her saddle and waved it at the cows. "Look what I have, guys. Cookies."

Cows swung in her direction, and dozens of liquid brown eyes brightened with cookie hopes. As she circled the car, the cattle bounded after her. The earth shook with the force of their powerful hooves.

"Next time, you're on your own, city boy." She tipped her hat. The cowgirl stayed on his mind, the sweetest thing he had ever seen.

Will Ford be able to stick it out in the country
to find out more about Autumn?
Find out in HIS HOLIDAY BRIDE
by bestselling author Jillian Hart,
available in October 2010
only from Love Inspired®.

BARBARA HANNAY

A Miracle for His Secret Son

Freya and Gus shared a perfect summer, until
Gus left town for a future that couldn't include
Freya.... Now eleven years on, Freya has a life-
changing revelation for Gus: they have a son,
Nick, who needs a new kidney—a gift only his
father can provide. Gus is stunned by the news,
but vows to help Nick. And despite everything,
Gus realizes that he still loves Freya.

**Can they forge a future together and
give Nick another miracle...a family?**

Available October 2010

HARLEQUIN®

INTRIGUE®

A MURDER MYSTERY LEADS TO A LOT
OF QUESTIONS. WILL THE ANSWERS BE
MORE THAN THIS TOWN CAN HANDLE?

FIND OUT IN THE EXCITING
THRILLER SERIES BY BESTSELLING
HARLEQUIN INTRIGUE AUTHOR

B.J. DANIELS

WHITEHORSE
MONTANA

Winchester Ranch Reloaded

BOOTS AND BULLETS
October 2010

HIGH-CALIBER CHRISTMAS
November 2010

WINCHESTER CHRISTMAS WEDDING
December 2010